The Fake Holidate

LILLIE JEAN ANDREWS

Also by

<u>Of Passions and Thrones: A Fantasy Romance series</u>

Book One: The Last Daughter of Smoke and Shadows

Book Two: The First Prince of Pain and Power

To all those looking for a warm hug during the holidays

CHAPTER ONE

ELLIE

S ome people adore going home for the holidays. Those people likely don't have a mother quite as overbearing as mine.

Sometimes I just wish she'd focus more on Brady. We're the same age, twins in fact, and yet, our mother consistently expresses her concerns about my dating life. I would be more than willing to bet Brady doesn't get almost weekly phone calls asking if he's met any new "suitors."

I get it, I don't exactly have the best track record, and I am getting "up there" in age but the last thing I need is the constant reminders of the lack of a ring on my finger.

Maybe that's why I lied. Maybe I just wanted a few weeks of peace, without my mothers pestering.

Telling your mom you're bringing home a date for Christmas? A mistake.

Telling your mom you're bringing home a date when you're so single your virginity has practically grown back? Even worse.

Not the best idea, but in my defense, I had planned on coming up with some sort of lie. Oh sorry, my mysterious new spouse is sick. Or maybe he had to run home to deal with a family emergency. Either way, I was not planning on showing up into Newberry without either a man on my arm or a good reason why he was not here.

And yet, I did it anyway.

The bright neon lights of Newberry's only bar almost blind me as I pull into their parking lot. My mother is not expecting me for another few hours so drowning at least a few of my sorrows seems like a good idea.

The sun just set and while I know there are actually quite a few residents in Newberry, it's surprising to see this many people crowded around the bar on a random Thursday night.

The bar, aptly named, Social Hour, is having a two-for-one special on anything mixed with Vodka. While Vodka isn't my drink of choice, a deals a deal.

After ordering, I scan the bar, not looking for anything special, it's just been over a year since I visited Newberry. Newberry isn't even that far from where I live, only a few hours drive, but it's the memories that keep me away.

My families overbearing opinions don't help.

I don't immediately spot anyone I recognize, which isn't surprising, Newberry is more a pass through, tourist type town than a spot you want to stop and start a family. Although they do have good festivals for every holiday, annual fairs and even a few half-way decent farmers markets, most attendees tend to come in from other neighboring towns.

I let my eyes wander over the Christmas lights bordering the door and a few of the grimy windows. It's not that I'm a grinch, though my coworkers at the bakery do enjoy calling me that, it's just that this particular holiday holds a lot of memories. Memories of my father, memories of my ex-fiancé.

Christmas is simply a loaded holiday for me.

Before I can dive too deeply into my thoughts, I hear the bartender place my first drink on the counter behind me. I turn, reaching into my back pocket intent on paying my bill and not turning it into a tab, I am driving after all, but the bartender stops me before I can give him the silver Amex in my hand.

"It's been paid for"

"By who?"

The bartender, who has such a large piercing though his septum it looks like it hurts, points to a shadowed corner I missed on my first glance.

"Thanks"

The bartender nods and walks away, leaving me sitting here wondering if I have to walk over and thank the man who bought the drink.

I'd rather not, but I suppose I'll have to deal with this sooner or later. I'll have to face my family, and those we hold close to us at some point today and I suppose if I'm going to do it, I'd rather start with the man sitting in the corner than jumping right into the deep end with someone like my mother or chosen aunt.

Grabbing my drink, I wade through the throngs of people towards my destination. Once I'm close enough, I stop and look up into those dark eyes.

"Thanks Benji" I say

Benjamin Harrison, my brothers best friend, someone I grew up with and someone I haven't spoken more than a few words to in almost two years.

"No problem"

Chapter Two

BENJI

I have to say, on the drive to Newberry, I hadn't given much thought as to whether Bradies sister would be attending this Christmas celebration but now that she's walking towards me, I can't help but wonder why I didn't.

Every year my parents, their best friend, and a few members of our extended family meet at what we all call the vacation houses. Two large, mansion style homes situated on a half-acre each and a clear, paved walking path between them.

It wasn't easy to get the two weeks my mother requested off but I know my sister is struggling, more than our mother knows and I'd do just about anything to lift her spirits. So when she called to make sure I was coming for the full two-week holiday break and not just the few days right at Christmas I usually try to get away with, how could I say no?

"Thanks Benji" Ellie says. She tips her drink slightly and climbs into the chair to my right. She's not the tallest and these are high top chairs but she manages it without issue.

"No problem" I tell her, "Glad to see you. I didn't realize you'd be here this year"

Somehow, she managed to get out of coming last year.

"Yeah, last year I couldn't get any time off of work. The bakery is always super busy this time of year but since I worked straight through Christmas last year, they let me take off this year. I might have to go back a few days early but we'll see."

She works as a baker at a mom-and-pop bakery in the city she lives in. I can't remember what city it is, but I don't think it's very far from where I'm at.

"How have you been?" I ask.

"Pretty good actually. Dreading being home and this holiday, but other than that, good. How about you?"

"I'm not bad. Looking forward to some time away from work and the holidays" Ellie nods along as I'm talking but

I can see some tension in her shoulders, "Why are you dreading being home?"

Ellie groans and tosses her head in her hands. Her brown hair pulls from over her shoulders and covers her face even further.

"What is it?" I ask again. I can't tell if what's bothering her is a serious issue that needs to be addressed or something more trivial.

Finally, she pulls her head out of her hands, takes another sip of her drink and says, "I told my mother I was bringing someone home this year"

She turns and meets my eyes. I'm not quite sure what the issue is, unless,

"Was that not true?"

She looks at me like I'm and idiot before answering. It does something to me I am not prepared for.

"Of course it's not true! I only told her that so she'd leave me alone about my dating life for a few weeks."

Yeah, I can see her logic. Our parents are the exact opposite of the "hands off" style of parenting. Thankfully my parents have both of my sisters to expend their energy on.

My oldest sister Elena has three kids that my parents adore being grandparents to and my youngest sister Carrie, their surprise baby, is in her senior year of high school. So between the two of them, I've been able to keep my head down and avoid the match making expertise of my mother. Ellie has clearly not been so lucky.

"You could just lie. Say he couldn't get off work or something" I offer to Ellie.

"I thought about it. But then they'd want to see pictures and what would I say to that?"

I grimace, "Yeah I can't help you there"

Ellie grumbles something under her breath and puts her forehead flat against the tabletop. I'd tell her I'm pretty sure they don't have a regular cleaning schedule here, but right now I feel like she has bigger problems.

"What am I going to do?"

I don't think she's actually asking as much as sharing her frustrations so I don't answer.

Everything is silent for a few minutes. It's weird, the two of us haven't really spoken except for the obligatory "happy birthday" texts we send each other but you'd never know it. I suppose growing up together gave us this level of familiarity but I won't lie and say I'm not a little disappointed in myself for not checking in with her more often.

I don't know how to solve Ellies problem. No matter what she chooses to do, there's likely to be some sort of consequence. Unless she can come up with a boyfriend in the next twenty minutes, I don't think she's going to be able to get out of this.

An idea comes to mind, but it sounds more insane than I care to admit.

Ellie finally lifts her head off the table. I see what might be a tear track and it grabs my heart in a vice grip. I haven't seen Ellie in almost two years, since the Christmas before last, but for some reason I'm feeling the inexplicable urge to solve her problems.

Time or no, Ellie is one of the people I care about and I can't stand to see them hurt. Maybe that's why, as insane as it sounds, an offer rolls off my tongue,

"What if I pretend to be your boyfriend?"

CHAPTER THREE

ELLIE

C rying in a bar in front of my brothers best friend and childhood crush is a rather weird end to my day. Benjamin Harrison, said childhood crush, offering to be my fake boyfriend is even weirder.

"What?" He needs to repeat himself because I'm not entirely sure I didn't hallucinate his offer.

"I'll pretend to be your boyfriend."

Even with him repeating himself, I'm not sure I'm hearing him right.

"Why would you do that?"

Benji shrugs, "It would be nice not to have my mother needle me about my relationship status. I can usually avoid her nosiness but the holidays always brings out her more meddlesome side."

"That's fair," I nod, "but what about Brady?" Brady is my twin brother and one of Benjis best friends. I don't know how he would feel at the prospect of me and Benji being in a relationship.

The fact that I'm even considering this, faking a relationship with my brothers best friend, is evidence of how desperate I am. Although teenage me would be practically vibrating with excitement. She had a huge crush on Benji that obviously never panned out. Adult me, however, is just about done with men in general.

Benji takes a moment before answering, "I guess there's a few ways we could handle that. We could pull him aside and tell him the truth or just see how he reacts to the idea."

I don't even know what to say. Sure, it would probably set off a few of my mothers alarms if I show up and announce Benji and I are dating but the alternative is showing up alone and I'm not sure I'm prepared to handle that.

Scratch that, I know I'm not prepared to handle that.

"Are you sure? I mean, we'd have to lie to our family. You've never shown any interest in me before so wouldn't it kind of throw them for a loop if we all of a sudden show up, arm in arm?"

Benjis answer is surprisingly quick, "Well, you did tell them you were bringing someone. I was seeing a woman a few months back that Elena knows about. I could just say that was you because they never actually met, nor did I give my sister any details."

"You're actually serious about this aren't you?" I'm still having trouble wrapping my head around the idea if I'm being honest.

Benji reaches over and turns my chin so I'm eye to eye with him, it sends a jolt somewhere that hasn't seen any proper action in years.

"I am Ellie. I want to help you"

I take a deep breath, seriously considering my options before I respond. Christmas music is playing lowly through the bars speaker system, it adds a bit of ambiance to the situation that helps move along my answer. I don't want to put Benji out but he seems fairly open to the idea and the last thing I want is to have to deal with my mothers "helpful" opinions and actions.

Mind made up, I announce,

"It's a deal, but first, we have to have rules"

I grab a napkin and a pen from over the counter and set to work

<u>Ellie & Benjis Rules for Fake Dating</u>
<u>-Written by Ellie</u>

-We only tell Brady of our lie

-The ruse ends two weeks after vacation
when we "break up"

-Open communication <u>always</u>

-If anyone starts to get suspicious,
deny deny deny!

-Minimal PDA

-<u>No</u> falling in love

-No matter what happens, we
will always be friends

Chapter Four

ELLIE

Before my father died, Christmas was my favorite time of year. It wasn't just the holiday itself, it was the entire season. The lights framing houses throughout the neighborhood, the winter festivals, picking out a tree, all of it.

Then, Christmas day seven years ago, my father had a heart attack and was gone before the clock struck midnight.

I know he would be disappointed to know that I've let my joy for the holiday season fall away but when you combine the death of your parent with finding out your fiancé cheated on you, both having happened on Christmas day, it seems more understandable.

That said, the vacation houses are glorious, especially during the holidays. Two large Mediterranean style homes situated on half-acre each. Our parents bought them over twenty years ago and have met here for each and every holiday since the purchase. There's a room for each of us, and plenty extras for the various cousins and friends who come to stay, and each is decorated to the point it looks like Santa threw up everywhere.

You wouldn't think a large house complete with candy canes lining the driveway, plastic light up reindeer and iridescent lights framing each and every window would be intimidating and yet, it definitely is.

"Just remember, they don't know we're lying and the only way they'll find out is if we tell them." Benji says, attempting to reassure me.

I've got our rule napkin tucked into my back pocket, a smile plastered on my face and as much fake confidence as I can muster. I don't think my mother will come right out and accuse us of lying, why would she, but I do expect her to have about a million questions, most of which I have no answer for.

"Are you sure?" I ask Benji, wanting to give him one last chance to back out.

"Yes," He says, "And even if I wasn't it's too late now"

I realize what he means when I look over and see my mom standing in the doorway, arms spread wide. My mom is a stout woman, five-three at best and I'm not much taller than her. Her normally dyed blonde hair is showing gray at its roots and if she took off the makeup on her face, I'd likely spy a few wrinkles and a small birthmark above her cheek.

"Ellie!" She screeches, running from the open doorway, down the porch stairs to where me and Benji are standing next to our cars.

"Mom!" I drop the bag I'm holding and wrap my arms around her. Even with all the stress she can cause me, I know, in my heart, that my mother loves me more than anything.

"How are you sweetie?" She asks in my ear, arms still wrapped tight around me.

"I'm great, happy to be here"

Finally, she releases me. She keeps her hands on my upper arms as she looks me over. I don't think I look any different than when she saw me about a month ago but mom eyes are a bit different.

Satisfied with whatever she sees, she takes a step back and looks around.

"Lovely to see you Benji," Mom steps up and wraps Benji in a hug. I don't know the last time they saw each other but I think it might have been last Christmas.

After my mom and Benji separate, she turns to me, "And where is your mystery man?"

I can feel a sheepish smile spread across my face.

"Actually," I begin to say. I don't get very far before Benji steps up beside me and grabs my hand.

I can see the confusion on my moms face. It would be funny if it wasn't so nerve-wracking. Her eyes linger on our joined hands and I can see the moment it clicks.

"Marsha!" She shouts, calling for Benjis mom.

And so it begins.

CHAPTER FIVE

BENJI

My hand is still burning where it held Ellies just a few moments ago. I don't know why, I'm sure we've been that close to each other before, but I can't seem to remember when.

"I think that went well, don't you?" Ellie asks from across the small room.

"As good as it could've I suppose"

After Ellies mom called mine outside, both women hounded us for answers about our "relationship" until something clattered in the kitchen through the open front door, pulling their attention away and giving us an opportunity to escape.

I'll admit, this might not have been my best idea and we definitely did not think this through before leaving the bar. Evidence of that is currently sitting in front of me.

Both mine and Ellies personal bags are spread out on the bed in front of me. The only bed.

I don't think I considered all the possible repercussions before making my offer to Ellie. I wouldn't take it back, but I do think we should have considered what the day to day would look like while in our so-called relationship. Sleeping arrangements being one of those things.

Ellie either hasn't noticed or simply doesn't care. She's been staring out the window since we came up here. Over-all, it could be worse. Our parents have stuck us in Ellies bedroom at the end of the hall on the second floor. We share a bathroom with her younger cousin, the connecting door on the wall behind me, but other than that, we're away from the majority of the family. Those who would be likely to sniff out our deal.

The bedroom is decent sized, with a queen bed in the middle of the wall and a bay window with a view of the front yard. There is not a closet but I didn't bring much to wear anyways, planning to open up my dresser with various Christmas sweaters and warm clothes in my room across the way.

I would have argued that I can stay in my room in my families house right next door but I didn't want to seem suspicious. We need this ruse to last the two weeks we'll be here and our mothers getting suspicious on day one does not bode well for us.

It takes a minute, but I finally work up the nerve to pull Ellie away from the window and focus on the problem quite literally sitting in front of me.

"What are we going to do about this?"

"About what?" Ellie asks, turning to look at me

I gesture to the bed, Ellie is only confused for a second before she understands my question.

"Oh," She comments.

"Yeah"

"Well," Ellie begins, walking over to me, "I could sneak up into the attic later. I think there's an old air mattress in storage up there."

"But wouldn't that look suspicious if someone were to walk in here? If we're in a relationship, why would one of us be sleeping on an air mattress"

"You're right" She tells me

It's silent for a few minutes, both of us simply staring at the bed. The idea of sleeping next to Ellie isn't weird to me but it does unsettle me in a way I can't identify. I can't tell if Ellie feels the same but she does seem a lot calmer than I'm feeling right now.

"We could say we're fighting" She offers

"And then everyone will want to know what about and try to fix it"

Ellie nods, "Then I guess we'll just have to share." She slaps her hands together, fishes a small bag out of her suitcase and walks into the attached bathroom.

I give the bed one last glare before digging out my toiletries and following her lead.

CHAPTER SIX

BENJI

The sun had just set when we left the bar but now it's definitely late. After unpacking a few of my belongings, I left Ellie alone to wander over to my families house intent on finding Elena.

On the short walk, I sent Brady a text to let him know to come and speak directly to me or Ellie before he assumes anything. The last thing I need right now is Brady pissed at me because he thinks I went behind his back to get with his sister.

When we were teens, Brady warned me away from Ellie. He made points like the fact that she's two years younger than me, I was always planning on moving out of our hometown and most importantly, she's Bradies sister and

Brady is my best friend. I don't know if the warning still stands but knowing Brady, I would bet it still does.

I find Elena where I expected to, cozied up on the large sectional couch watching a Christmas movie. I toss myself down next to her and tug the blanket away from her to cover myself.

"Hey!" She reaches over to rip back the blanket and smacks the back of my head.

After taking the blanket back, Elena positions it in a way so that it's covering both of us.

"How are you?" I ask. I talked to her earlier this week but things seem to change in her life very quickly.

"I'm alright" She replies. I know it's a lie but I'm not going to call her on it.

"Where's Dave?" Dave is her deadbeat baby daddy, although if she heard me call him that I'd likely earn another smack to the back of the head.

Elena sighs, "He's upstairs sleeping. I put the kids down about an hour ago and he was asleep before then"

I don't respond, just hum to myself. Elena hears the message anyway.

"He had a full day at work yesterday. Everybody gets tired." I don't disagree but when you've got a wife and three kids, you need to learn to occasionally function while tired.

"I don't want to hear it" She argues, still picking up on what I'm not saying.

"I won't push, you know that. But I will remind you every day that you deserve better."

"Yeah yeah, I've heard it all before. Enough about me, what is this I hear about you showing up, hand in hand with Ellie?"

My cheeks burn. I don't want to lie to Elena but she tends to be inclined to tell Carrie everything, even the things I ask her not to. And if Carrie knows, then it will certainly get back to my parents.

"You knew I was seeing someone" I tell her, referring to the woman I dated for only a few weeks a couple months back. It wasn't Ellie but Elena doesn't need to know that.

"Yeah I just didn't realize it was Bradies sister. How'd he take it?"

I cringe, "I haven't told him yet" Brady gets here first thing in the morning so at least Ellie and I didn't have to deal with both our mothers and Brady right when we got here.

Elena sucks in a breath, "How do you think he'll take it?"

"I think it'll be fine. We're both adults and at this point there's not much he can do about it"

"So it's going well then?"

I really hate lying to Elena and there hasn't been much I've had to keep from her over the years, but I can't risk our mothers finding out.

"Yes," I tell her, "It's going really good"

"Then I'm happy for you" She rests her head on my shoulder. I wish she'd dump that husband of hers and find someone who actually deserves her but now's definitely not the time to bring it up, it would only ruin this little slice of peace she's found down here on the couch.

"So how's the sex?" Elena asks after a few minutes, forever the big sister enjoying her younger brothers discomfort.

I groan, "We're not talking about that"

Elena laughs and the sound grips my heart. "Fine, I don't really want to know anyways but you will be answering some of my other questions."

"And that's my cue" I respond, standing up off the couch. Ellie and I haven't really had the time to come up with all the little details I know everyone is going to ask about. We barely got away from our mothers earlier without giving away too much or contradicting ourselves.

"Run away all you want," Elena calls after me, "But I want to hear all about your relationship"

I leave the house, heading back to Ellie and our shared room. How I wish I didn't have to lie to my sister. This is turning out to be harder than I expected.

Chapter Seven

ELLIE

Sleeping naked has never been an issue for me before. Now that I'm sharing a bed with Benji, going commando doesn't seem like the best idea.

I showered right after Benji left. My younger cousin Allie will be here sometime in the next few days, so I took the time to enjoy our shared bathroom space without her million and one products littering it. That led me here, standing in front of the bed wrapped in a towel with my suitcase wide open.

My only option is my festive Christmas pajamas my mother insists we bring every year so that we can take a matching holiday picture. Those would be fine except that I've filled out a bit since my mother purchased them five years ago, meaning they're only comfortable for the five or so minutes it takes to snap the picture and move on.

I have a few bulky sweaters I could toss on, and pair of leggings but then I wouldn't have them to wear during the day.

Resigned, I snatch up the pajama set and make my way back into the bathroom. By the time I'm done, Benji is back. He's sorting through his bag and placing some of his clothes in the dresser we agreed to share.

It hasn't quite hit me yet that I'll be sharing my room with Benji. I know we discussed it earlier but talking about it and seeing it are two very different things.

I will admit though, it's nice to be sharing a space with someone I trust, even if it's not exactly like the others in this house think. The last time I shared this room was with my ex. I had already had some suspicions about his loyalty before the holidays. Then when I came back from a day of shopping to find him taking inappropriate pictures of himself I knew were not for me, my suspicions were confirmed.

Not wanting to make a fuss around the holidays, I spent the next week sharing this space with him. I haven't slept next to anyone since.

I hear Benji say something about taking a shower and I'll admit, I'm not paying much attention. Trying to bring myself out of my head, I climb onto the bed, snuggle into my pillow on the side closest to the window and close my eyes. If I could fall asleep before Benji gets out of the shower and avoid the awkwardness that will likely come, that would be great.

Unfortunately, I'm not that lucky.

I'm still wide awake when Benji exits the bathroom. I turn, finding him in loose plaid sleep pants and a cotton T-Shirt.

"Still awake?" He asks lowly

"Yeah"

"No wonder, you've still got the overhead light on"

"I didn't want it to be dark when you got out of the shower"

He smiles but it looks a bit forced, "Thanks"

It's quiet for a few minutes, Benji putting the clothes he was wearing in the hamper in the corner of the room and turning out the light. He gets into bed next to me and it's all I can do to try to ignore the warmth radiating from him. Even turned, facing away from him, his sheer presence in the room is impossible to ignore.

"It's actually good you're still awake. We need to talk about a few things."

I roll over, finding Benji closer than I expected. Trying not to make him uncomfortable, I sit up and lean against the headboard. He does the same.

"What is it?" I ask, the low lighting in the room making it feel like I need to whisper.

"We need to get our stories straight. People are going to have questions and I want to make sure we give them the right answers."

"Okay, what were you thinking?" I have a few ideas as to the questions people will ask and I hadn't yet come up with answers so it's good we're talking about this.

"How about we start with how this whole thing started?" Benji angles his body towards me. Northern Virginia is cold this time of year so I want to blame the temperature outside on the feeling of wanting to snuggle into him, but I'm pretty sure I'd be lying.

"That's an easy one," I tell him, "Say you came into the bakery one day and we got to talking. Everything spiraled from there."

Benji nods, "That's good. What's the bakery you work at called again?"

"It's called Sugar Rush. I've been working there the past five years as a head baker."

"What town is it in?"

"I'm in Oakville. You're in Davenport right?"

"Yes I am. How'd you remember that?"

I shrug, "Not sure, probably just heard it in passing one day and it stuck"

"Wait, so if you're in Oakville, that's less the forty-five minutes from me. That's not far at all"

Nodding, I tell him, "I hadn't really thought about it like that before. I actually go into Davenport sometimes to shop or just spend the day. I'm surprised we haven't run into each other."

"I just can't believe we've been so close to each other all this time" Benji is giving me a look I can't decipher in the darkness. Wanting to move the conversation along, I ask,

"Okay so what other parts of the story do we need to decide on?"

Benji says something I hadn't even thought about and we spend the next ten minutes talking about how to fit it into our lie. We spend most of the night like that, sitting next to each other in the darkness, coming up with stories no one should ever find out are lies. We talk until it's almost early morning hours and we're both so exhausted we don't have the brain power to keep coming up with things. At least, nothing that makes sense.

I fall asleep facing Benji, and he drifts off not long after me.

CHAPTER EIGHT

BENJI

I wake to a sudden scream. Instantly alert, I find the intruder only moments after my eyes open.

"Fuck, Brady!" Ellie exclaims. I've never heard her curse before and it's actually kind of adorable.

Moving on to the problem, I sit up hoping Ellie did not realize I had practically wrapped my entire body around her in my sleep.

"Someone needs to fill me in before I boil one of you alive" Brady says, sitting at the foot of our bed. I don't know how long he's been there but of all the faces I've woken up to over the years, his is probably my least favorite right now.

Ellie groans and throws herself back down on the bed.

"Couldn't you wait until we were up before barging in here? You're disturbing my rest!" Ellies tone is very scolding but it doesn't seem to bother Brady.

"You two are disturbing my entire holiday!" Brady says, wiggling into the bed between us, "Not only did you go behind my back and start dating, but I have to hear it from Carrie?"

"Relax you big baby," Ellie tells him, "We're not actually dating"

"What?" Brady demands, pushing me over so he can get comfortable.

"Tell him Benji, I'm going back to sleep" Ellie rolls away from us and pulls the blanket back over her head.

"What Ellie said is true. We're not actually dating."

"Then why do our entire joined families think you are?" I can't tell if Brady is pissed off or hurt and I don't know which would be worse. He rolls towards me and if it weren't for the fact I've know the guy and been friends with him our entire lives, I wouldn't care enough to explain.

"We are just pretending to date," I start to explain, "To get our parents off our backs about our lives and to actually be able to get some peace and quiet during the holidays"

Brady considers, "Is this true?" he asks Ellie, poking her through the blanket.

"Fuck off," She tells him, "But yes. And you can't tell anyone"

"Hmm," Brady considers, "Well I'm glad I don't have to beat you up for going behind my back to get with my sister"

I suppose that means his "no dating Ellie" rule from our teen years is still in place.

"Now why don't you go downstairs and get breakfast started" Brady tells me, practically forcing me off the bed.

"Fine" I slip out from under the covers and Brady immediately takes my spot. I think maybe I'll put some onion powder in his omelet, an allergic reaction would serve him right for kicking me out of bed.

I hear Brady and Ellie bickering as I leave the room. It sounds like I'm not the only one being kicked out of bed. I smile as I make my way down into the kitchen. Brady can be the biggest pain in the ass when he wants to be but man have I missed him.

***

I make everyone in the house omelets, unfortunately not poisoning Brady, but by the time everyone is awake, half of them are cold. I don't really mind, it's enjoyable to me to be able to make something with my hands. My work in the IT department for a large company doesn't usually allow for much hands-on work. It's nice to be able to create every so often.

Ellie is one of the first to come downstairs and I immediately hand her a plate.

"How's the bed hog?" I ask her.

"Fine," She tells me, "Annoying and still asleep in our bed but I didn't realize how much I'd missed him"

"I get that" It sends an unusual feeling through my stomach to hear her refer to "our bed."

Finishing off the last omelet, I take my plate and sit down next to her. No one else is up yet and it's the perfect time to ask her about todays plan.

"Did Brady agree to keep quiet?"

"Yes. He actually thinks our plan is pretty smart."

I nod along, "Speaking of the plan, what's on the agenda for today?"

"My mom has asked for help going into town to do some Christmas gift shopping and I said I'd accompany her"

I'm about to ask if she needs to go over the story we created before she heads out with her mom when someone enters the kitchen.

It turns out to be Carrie, followed by Ellie's and mines moms.

"How are our two lovebirds this morning?" Ellies mom asks, walking up and hugging Ellie from behind.

"Don't call us that" Ellie groans.

"Why not? It's cute!" Ellies mom lets go of her and walks over to pick up one of the various omelets I have plated.

"When do you want to leave mom?" Ellie asks, effectively changing the subject. I watch my little sister and mother pick out plates and then carry them off into the living room.

"Well since we don't have to drop by the fire station to leave some cookies and check out the eligible bachelors, I'd say around nine."

I don't know if Ellies mom is kidding about the whole "eligible bachelors" thing or not but based off the look on Ellies face, I'd say she's not.

Ellies mom leaves the room with her food, leaving me and Ellie alone. As soon as she's gone, Ellie gives me a look that tells me we are doing the exact right thing by pretending to be in a relationship.

If neither Ellie nor I have to wander the streets of Newberry with our incredibly overbearing mothers looking for someone to enter into a relationship with, then I'd say this fake relationship is exactly what we needed.

Chapter Nine

ELLIE

I love my mother, I truly do, but the woman does not understand the phrase "tone it down." She does everything on her highest setting. As someone who prefers to chill out fairly regularly, sometimes just watching her exhausts me.

I'm currently sitting across from her at one of the little cafes on main street. The trunk of my car is full of presents and we're not even halfway through her list.

"Next I want to stop by the quilting store to get some fabric for Elena" My mom takes a sip of her hot chocolate, I watch her go over the list we've already gone over twice.

Ignoring her statement to focus on something more important, I ask, "Are you alright mom?"

She glances at me, a little furrow in her brow, "Of course honey, why wouldn't I be?"

"I just know this time of year can be hard" I don't specifically mention dad but she gets the message anyway.

"It was hard at first," She admits, "And I miss your father every single day and likely will for the rest of my life. But now it's one of the few times during the year we are all together so it's hard to be sad when I have my favorite people around me."

I don't think she meant to weigh me down but her statement does nonetheless, I don't visit her as much as I should. We're only a few hours apart by car but in the past couple of months I've only made the trip twice. Once for Thanksgiving and once for a random pop in when I was already headed this way for something else.

"I know I don't visit as often as I should"

"Nonsense!" Mom reaches across the table and takes both of my hands in hers, "You're a busy girl. I know that. And I'm sure Benji has been keeping you busy"

I force a smile to my face, "Yeah he has." I don't like lying but I also don't like hearing all about how my single life saddens my mother. I know I'm almost thirty-four, I know my fertility declines as I get older, I know my mom wants to see me in a white dress, but I'd like to not be reminded of all that and simply enjoy the holidays as best I can.

"Tell me more about your relationship" Mom squeezes my hands before letting them go.

"What do you want to know?"

"Well, is he treating you right?"

"Of course he is mom, it's Benji"

"You never know" Mom shrugs, "Your last boyfriend seemed like an angel"

"I'd rather not talk about him"

"Fair enough, why don't you tell me a little about your relationship? I just want to know that you're happy"

I try to keep the story and details Benji and I came up with last night in my head. It would be very easy to stray off on a tangent that could end up with us getting caught.

"He makes me breakfast every morning we're together," I start. It seems reasonable considering he made everyone in the house breakfast this morning.

"That's nice"

"Most of the time we simply hang out together on the couch at my house. We watch a lot of old Disney movies and by the time morning comes, he's made me coffee and gotten everything ready for me to leave the house." I always leave super early to get to the bakery on time and sometimes my mornings can be stressful rushing out the door, something my mother knows.

I don't know where these words are coming from but if I'm being honest, the scenario is definitely something I could see Benji fulfilling.

"What about the more serious stuff? Have you guys talked about the future? Moving in together and kids?"

I groan, "Mom, we've only been dating a few months. It's a little early for that"

"Oh come on," She counters, "It's Benji, you've known him your whole life"

"That's true," I respond, "But I've only known him in the capacity of my boyfriend for a few months. It's different than simple friendship"

"Does that mean you don't see a future with him?"

"No mom, it's just that we're adjusting to our new positions in each others lives. I'm sure talk of the future will come"

Mom hums and I think that's the end of our conversation, at least until we finish our pastries and start to head outside.

"Do you know if Benjamin wants kids?"

"Why don't you ask him" I respond and walk away.

I'm starting to wonder if we're doing the right thing faking this relationship. My mind runs as I get into the car, at least it does until a firetruck rolls by and I remember my mothers words from this morning and suddenly, I'm positive Benji and I made a good decision.

CHAPTER TEN

ELLIE

My mother would be pleased to know she got in my head. The entire rest of the shopping trip and the drive back to the house I couldn't stop wondering about what Benji wants out of his future. Is there a reason he hasn't gotten married? Does he want kids and if so, how many?

My thoughts follow me up the stairs, towards my bedroom where I intend to drop off the few items I bought while shopping today.

I struggle to get the door open with the bags in my hands but when I do, the sight waiting for me startles me so badly I drop most of them.

"Sorry!" I shout, turning around.

I just walked in on Benji. More specifically, I just walked in on Benji naked, his bare butt being the first sight in the room when I opened the door.

From what I saw, it looked like he was changing his clothes. I don't know why he'd do that in the middle of the day or why he didn't seem to be putting on boxers but here we are.

From the other side of the door I hear a rustling and then a faint curse.

"It's alright" Benji calls, "You can come in now"

"Are you decent?"

I hear a low chuckle and then, "Yeah you're good"

I slowly open the door, trusting Benjis words but a little nervous after what just happened. Thankfully by the time I get the door open after picking up the fallen bags, Benji is fully dressed.

"Sorry," I repeat, "I guess I should've knocked. I just didn't realize you'd be up here"

"No need to be sorry," Benji says somewhat sheepishly, "It's your room. I spilled milk on my pants trying to make cookies with Carrie. I would've changed in the bathroom but I thought you'd be gone a little while longer."

"It's fine" I want to move on from this awkward experience. I've seen men naked before, obviously, but none of them were Benji.

My cheeks feel flush and despite the cold, I feel rather warm as I place my shopping bags down in the corner of the room. Wanting to change the subject and move on from what just happened, I ask the first question that comes to mind,

"Do you want kids?"

Benji looks startled at the abrupt change in subject. I'll admit, not my finest moment. I hadn't planned on asking him, but seeing his naked backside has thrown me for a loop. Plus, if I actually think about it, since we're supposed to be in a relationship, it's probably something I should know.

"Um," Benji pauses, thinking, and sits down on the edge of the bed.

"You don't have to answer if you don't want to. It's just, my mother asked earlier today and I think she got in my head more than I realized." I walk over and sit next to him.

"No, no it's a good question. If we're apparently dating, then we should probably know that about each other"

"My thoughts exactly"

"I do," Benji starts, "I didn't always and as I've gotten older, the idea seems more impossible but I do think I'd really love to have a couple of little ones running around one day. With the right person of course."

"Why haven't I ever seen you with someone for more than a few months before?" It seems odd that a man like Benji, kind and successful, would be single for so long.

"I guess I just haven't found the right person yet" Benji turns towards me and we make eye contact. He holds it for longer than I would've expected before breaking it to glance down at my lips.

For a second, only a second, I think he might want to kiss me. For that second, I think I want him to kiss me.

The moment is broken when a loud crash followed by someone shouting, "I'm okay!" echoes from downstairs.

We break apart. I didn't realize quite how close we'd gotten.

"Do you um," Benji scratches the back of his neck, "Do you want kids?"

I nod, "I do. I always have but like you said, the older I get, the more it starts to become unrealistic." My voice comes out weaker than I'd like. I can't tell if it's because of what just happened or the subject matter.

"You'll have that one day," Benji tells me, finally looking back towards me, "You'd make an amazing mom. I believe in you."

"Thanks Benji" I smile, "I really hope you're right"

Chapter Eleven

BENJI

Ellie left the room ten minutes ago and I can't seem to move from this spot sitting at the edge of the bed.

I almost kissed her. I almost kissed Ellie, my childhood friend, my best friends sister and someone who, up until now I had never considered romantically.

I think maybe it was fear of losing my friendship with Brady that kept me from considering Ellie in the first place. By the time I started to grow out of that, to understand that both Brady and I were grown adults and I would not lose him from something like that as long as I was serious and never hurt her, Ellie and I had both gone away to college.

Then she met Harry.

Harry seemed like the epitome of a "nice guy." Always held doors open for Ellie, I could always see her smile when he was around, held her through the death of her father. He seemed perfect for her. Then we found out the "nice guy" wasn't so nice and had been cheating on her almost their entire relationship.

There is only one time in my life I have ever considered murder. It wasn't when Scott St. James picked on me freshman year of high school. It wasn't when, in college, a friend of mine tried to sleep with my girlfriend. I haven't even considered it with Dave, my sisters husband. Although he comes in close second.

The only time in my life I have ever considered murder was finding out, on Christmas day, that Ellies boyfriend of several years was cheating. I watched her heart break in real time that year and have held a grudge against anyone named Harry ever since.

My phone buzzes on the bed next to me and I pick it up. I open it to see a picture of Lucy, my cat, sent from my neighbor who I asked to look in on her. Lucy showed up in the dumpster outside my apartment building a little over a year ago and never left. The little shit attacked me several times when I tried to take the trash out. Then winter hit and I couldn't stand the idea of her being out in the cold so I went down, tossed a towel over her to keep her from clawing me and brought her inside.

She's been there ever since.

I send a quick heart emoji in response to the picture and stand up. I need to get out of this room, which has so many reminders of Ellie that if I want to try getting her, and the idea of kissing her, out of my mind, this is the worst place to do it.

I'm not entirely sure why I feel the need to run away from the idea of kissing Ellie. Maybe it's because I still have lingering worries about Brady or maybe I'm worried about screwing something up with someone I already love so much, but either way, I don't think I need to be having these thoughts and certainly do not need to be acting on them.

I walk back over to my parents house, finding Carrie where I left her, in the kitchen working on the cookies. I told her after we made such a big mess spilling the gallon of milk that maybe baking isn't in the cards for us, but she seems determined.

"How's it going?" I call out

"Good, I'm almost ready to put them in the oven."

I can see the little round dough balls she's placed on a cookie sheet. I quickly check the temperature of the oven and tell her it's ready.

After placing the cookie sheet in the oven, Carries turns to me and says,

"Perfect, now all we have to do is wait. What could go wrong?"

Turns out, a lot can go wrong.

All it takes it one decision to go outside, to help our father with the Christmas decorations he's attempting to put up, and one forgotten phone for everything to go wrong.

A while later we're outside, wrapping the banisters with tinsel when I ask,

"Carrie, what time is it? I feel like we've been out here long enough, but I haven't heard the timer on your phone"

Carrie reaches into her back pocket and immediate panic spreads across her face.

"Shit!" She curses, earning a scold from dad. It doesn't matter though because we're both abandoning what we were doing to rush inside, into the kitchen.

"Shit, shit, shit" Carrie keeps repeating. She grabs an oven mitt, rips oven the oven door and pulls out what looks like the pieces of coal Santa gives to bad kids.

The entire kitchen is filling with smoke. With no other options, I push open the window over the sink, letting in the cold air and turn on the range hood over the stove.

My hopes of the smoke detector not going off are quickly squashed.

Our dad has wandered in thanks to all the commotion. He quickly sees the issue and grabs a hand towel to begin fanning the smoke outside. Carrie and I follow in his lead.

"I think in the future we should leave the baking to Ellie" Our dad says to both of us.

I'm a thirty-five year old man but I feel about eight years old when he uses that scolding tone on me. I know he's not truly mad but I can't help it.

"Agreed" Both me and Carrie say.

Chapter Twelve

ELLIE

I don't want to start seeing Benji differently, I really don't. It would complicate things to a degree I'm not sure either of us could handle. With that said, I can't always control my brain.

Completing my bedtime routine next to him, standing at the sink, both of us brushing our teeth, me combing through my hair and him setting out his razor and shaving cream to shave off his stubble in the morning, it's all feeling too domestic.

I can't tell if it's lust because I haven't had good sex in years, or if I'm developing actual feelings for the guy. After his words earlier today, I'm worried it's the latter.

Thankfully Benji does not catch me staring at him as he climbs into his side of the bed. He does, however, catch me fidgeting with the uncomfortable sleeve of my Christmas pajamas.

"Is something wrong with your shirt?" He asks.

"No, it's just that these are the only pajamas I brought and they more for pictures than actually sleeping in so they're not the most comfortable"

"Oh," Benji considers for a second, "Let me grab you a T-shirt. That way you can be more comfortable"

"That's not necessary" The last thing I need is to be surrounded in Benjis scent after the way I've been feeling.

I need to remind myself that this relationship is not real, even when it feels like it. At the end of the holiday break, we will both be going back to our separate houses and probably won't see each other until the next holiday we come to the vacation houses for.

"No really, I insist" Benji reaches into the dresser on his side of the bed and pulls out a faded red T-shirt. He hands it to me and I start chanting in my head, "not real, not real"

"Are you sure?"

"Yeah," He nods, "You need good sleep to be dealing with our families all day everyday and for that, you need to be comfortable"

"Okay, thanks" And with that, I walk into the bathroom to change. By the time I'm done, Benji has turned off the lights and climbed into bed. I get in on the other side, making sure to stay as far away as I can without being suspicious.

"Night" I tell him

"Goodnight Ellie"

***

I can hear the crinkle of a condom wrapper. The weight of a chest presses down hard on top of me.

"Benji!" I moan

"That's it," He tells me, "Come on my cock Ellie"

The room is dark, leaving no room for sight, only feelings, and I'm feeling about a million things right now.

It feels like every nerve ending in my body is firing off at the same time. The slow drag of Benji moving inside of me, the pressure of his weight on my chest and his body rubbing against my clit, it's all too much.

"Oh god" I'm screaming now

Benji chuckles, "I knew you'd feel like perfection"

***

I wake sweaty, frustrated and embarrassed. It's been a long time since I had a sex dream, years even. It has to be latent sexual frustration from my last relationship combined with being around an attractive and kind man like Benji. My only hope is that I didn't make any noises or movements that would have given me away.

I look over my shoulder towards Benji, finding him laying with his back towards me.

"Benji?" I whisper, not wanting to wake him if he's still sleeping. I can tell it's early morning by the light coming in through the window. Likely not as late as I usually wake up but still a reasonable time to be awake.

"Yeah?" His voice is gravelly and rough. It's not a tone I'm used to hearing from him.

"Just checking to see if you were awake" I respond. I cannot tell if Benji knows what I was dreaming about or not.

"I'm up, just laying here"

"Okay. I think I'm going to get up and head downstairs." I sit up in bed, Benji makes no move from his position facing away from me. I think my best course of action here is to pretend the dream never happened, it's not obvious whether Benji noticed what I was dreaming about so I'm hoping that means he didn't.

"You okay?" I ask, noting he hasn't turned towards me yet.

"Yeah, all good. I think I might just sleep for a while longer."

"Alright" I ease out of bed, "Let me know if you need anything" I can't tell if he's simply tired, not feeling good or uncomfortable because he knows about my dream.

He's just tired, I tell myself, just tired.

Chapter Thirteen

BENJI

Her moans might be the sweetest sounds I've ever heard.

I woke up sometime late last night or early this morning to Ellie rubbing against me.

Again, I had migrated to her side of the bed in my sleep and wrapped myself around her like a koala. I was just thankful she hadn't woken up and noticed me up against her. That was, until I heard her moaning my name.

I'm not a stranger to sex. I've been in various relationships over the years, sometimes casual, sometimes more. They never panned out but they did give me a sort of comfort around sex.

That said, I've never responded to another person the way I did to Ellie. I know I should have gotten up, left the room or at least put a pillow to my ears instead of lying there listening to her, but I couldn't help it. And when she moaned my name, I about levitated off the bed.

My dick has been rock solid since I woke up and now it's bordering on painful. It's why I couldn't face Ellie when she finally did wake up, ceasing her enchanting sounds. I couldn't let her see what was going on in my pants. Then she'd know for sure I heard her and likely be uncomfortable.

I think I've been developing feelings for Ellie since she walked back into my life in that bar only a few days ago but today they seem so much larger than yesterday.

I hear Ellies footsteps on the stairs down the hall and decide it's time to get up.

I have two choices, a freezing cold shower to try to will away the issue, or I could take care of it and be done. I know I shouldn't jerk off to Ellie, my childhood friend, my best friends sister and someone who I will be leaving in just a few weeks but I don't think I can help it.

Who knows, maybe it will even help get rid of these feelings I'm having, or at least lessen them. Kind of like a "getting it out of my system" sort of thing.

At least, that's what I'm telling myself as I enter the bathroom and drop my pants. I lean over the toilet to take care of the mess afterwards and get started.

The first touch to my dick nearly sends me into orbit.

I grasp myself hard and rough. I can get this done quickly, I know I can. I'm chaffing a bit and in a bout of insanity, I lean over and grab just a small bit of Ellies hand lotion off the sink counter.

I'm crossing a line here, I know that, but I can't bring myself to stop. I start imaging putting Ellie in all sorts of positions, on her knees, on her back and on top of me. I think she'd like being on top, being in control. Or maybe she wouldn't, maybe she'd want me to press her hard into the mattress, to nearly suffocate her with my weight as I thrust in and out of her.

"Ellie," I groan out. I'm nearly there, just a few more strokes and I can be done with this whole thing.

Chapter Fourteen

ELLIE

The house is chilly and quiet when I get downstairs. I look on the couch for one of my sweaters, or even a blanket to wrap myself in. I'm not quite hungry yet so I think I'll just put on a movie and wait for the rest of the house to awaken.

The one good thing about the cold is that it chills my heated blood. Remnants of my dream from last night keep playing over and over in my head, giving me no escape.

Thinking about sex and Benji in the same context can lead nowhere good.

After my last relationship, the one that ended in finding out he cheated on Christmas day, I wasn't sure I would ever have these feelings again. Harry somewhat ruined men for me. I don't mind admiring them from afar but anything more and I'd rather just keep things platonic. That way they can't hurt me.

Unfortunately, keeping every available man I've ever known at arms length is not conducive to a very vibrant sex life. Which is fine. If I'm being honest, things had gotten rather drab with Harry, even before I found out about the cheating. That fact alone tells me that even if I were to let a man in, it likely wouldn't be as amazing as the romance books tell you. If I can't even have good sex with a man I'd been in love with and heavily attracted to, why would anyone else be different?

Somehow, I don't feel like that would be an issue with Benji. Now that I've sort of let myself look and think about him in that way, I can easily say that the man looks like sex on a stick.

Shaking my head as if trying to physically purge my thoughts from my brain, I go back on the hunt for something to keep me warm. Virginia winters can be harsh when they want to be.

Not finding even a throw blanket on the couch, all of them likely haven been stolen by Elenas kids for a fort, I decide to head back upstairs to grab a sweater so I can be comfortable.

I'm trying to be quiet as I approach my room. Benji said he was going to go back to sleep and I don't want to wake him.

Easing the door open, I find the bed empty and the covers thrown back. There's a soft light coming from under the bathroom door which tells me where Benji is. It's providing enough of a glow for me to spot a large sweatshirt of mine on the floor near my nightstand. I likely took it off after shopping yesterday and tossed it down.

I grab the sweatshirt and turn to leave. I'm about to open the door and head back downstairs when I hear a low groan followed by my name.

Pausing for a moment, I'm about to dismiss what I heard when my name comes again. I quickly move over to the bathroom door where I hear my name for the third time.

Remembering that Benji seemed unwell earlier, I grasp the bathroom door handle and throw open that door, thinking Benji might be hurting and needing help.

The sight that greets my eyes is not what I expected.

"Ahh!" I screech and reach for the bathroom door to shut it. Benji makes eye contact with my for only a second before I have the door slammed shut.

This is the second time I've walked in on Benji almost completely naked. Except this time, he had his penis in his hand and was vigorously getting himself off.

"Sorry!" I call, "I heard my name and thought you might need help!"

Benji doesn't respond so I quickly scramble over to the bedroom door and open it to leave.

"I'm leaving," I call to Benji, wanting to give him his privacy. Again, I get no response.

I'm all the way back downstairs when I stop to actually realize what just happened. I just walked in on Benjamin Harrison masturbating. Not only was he masturbating but if his words are any indication, he was doing it to thoughts of me.

Chapter Fifteen

ELLIE

I'm pacing around the living room, cold, seeing as I dropped my sweater when I opened the door on Benji and didn't realize. I've got a Christmas movie playing on the large television but I can't sit still long enough to watch it. It's been playing for about ten minutes, but I couldn't tell you a word about what's happening.

That tends to happen when you walk in on your brothers best friend, your fake boyfriend, masturbating to thoughts of you. Or at least, I would assume it does.

I hear someone coming down the stairs and quickly toss myself onto the couch, attempting to look the picture of ease and comfort.

It's not Benji who emerges from down the hall and I'm almost glad it isn't. I have no idea what's going to happen when he finally comes out of our room. Are we going to talk about it? Are we just going to ignore what happened and brush it under the rug? And which would I prefer to happen?

"You okay?" Brady asks, walking by me to go into the kitchen.

"Peachy" I tell him.

"Sure you are" Brady stops and turns to where I'm sitting on my hands to keep from fiddling with them. He sits down next to me and does not say a word.

"Are you okay Brady?"

"I'm great, just wondering when you're going to tell me what has you acting so weird"

Like hell would I tell Brady that I just walked in on his best friend with his dick in his hand.

"I don't think I'm acting weird"

"Your back is ramrod straight, you're sitting on the edge of the couch, and you have your hands tucked under your thighs to keep from fidgeting. Did something happen with Benji? If so, I'll kill him."

I'm usually thankful Brady and I are close, but when he uses that twin sense to read me when I really don't want him too, I kind of wish we had been separated at birth.

"Benji didn't do anything wrong" Technically, it's not a lie. I don't think I'd characterize Benji jerking off while saying my name as "wrong." I just don't know what to characterize it as and I think that's what's throwing me off.

"Okay, so what's the problem?"

I look to Brady. He may get on my nerves more often than not, but I truly love him and know I can trust him to keep my secrets. We wouldn't have told him the truth about our relationship otherwise.

"I'm having confusing feelings about Benji" That seems like the best way to put it.

"Confusing as in, you like him, or confusing as in, you'd like to throw him out a window?"

"The first"

Brady groans, "I knew this would happen! Just like I knew when you had a crush on him in high school and tried to hide it"

I reach over a grab a pillow. I hit him with it but otherwise make no response. Brady takes the pillow from me and tosses it behind him.

"What does Benji say?"

"I haven't said anything," I tell him, but after last night and this morning I have a feeling he knows, "I've known him for so long. Is it weird?" Thankfully I don't have to elaborate.

"To me, yes it's very weird. You are my sister and he's my best friend. It's very low on the list of things I want to think about."

I wish I still had the pillow to hit him again.

"On the other hand," Brady hesitates before he ultimately continues his statement, "Benji is one of the best guys that I know. After Harry, you deserve someone who will treat you right."

"And you think Benji is that guy?"

"I don't know Ellie. I think the only person who can answer that is you."

"I haven't had these feelings long enough to really think about it"

"Well then, maybe pause before you change something you can't take back. I don't want to be stuck missing one of you every holiday because you're too uncomfortable to be in the same room as each other."

"Thanks Brady" I lean my head on his shoulder, finally feeling relaxed for the first time since I woke up this morning.

"Just talk to him" Brady tells me quietly, "And restart the movie so I can watch it too"

I lean over and grab the remote, intent on doing exactly that.

Chapter Sixteen

BENJI

By the time I gather the courage to go downstairs and face Ellie, the sun has almost fully risen and I can hear others moving around downstairs.

I don't know if she's going to be mad or disgusted with me. It's pretty obvious what I was doing, and who's name I was calling out while I was doing it.

I don't think I can handle if Ellie is upset with me. She's always been important to me but recently she's begun to become one of the most important. I want to think she'll be okay with what happened but so far, I haven't picked up on much, if any, interest towards me other than her dream last night which was pretty much against her will.

I can smell something baking when I come downstairs. I spot Ellie and Brady on the couch with what looks to be a Christmas movie I've never seen before playing on the TV. I make my way past them, unable to look at Ellie, and into the kitchen to find Ellies mother pulling muffins out of the oven.

"Good morning Celia."

"Good morning Benji, sleep well?" Brady and Ellies mother asks.

I was until her daughter rubbed against me and set off a series of events that led to her walking in on me naked for the second time, but I'm not going to tell her that.

"I did, thank you. What are you making?"

"Blueberry muffins, would you like one?"

"No thanks" I'm nervous about talking to Ellie and I don't think adding something to my stomach would be the best idea.

I'm afraid to ruin the relationship between us. Our plan has been working and I would hate to be the one to bring it all down. I should've thought about that before I wrapped my hand around my dick.

Brady wanders into the kitchen to snag one of his mothers muffins. She tells him to bring them over to my parents' house so we can all have breakfast over there. Brady follows her orders and walks out the back door. Celia is not far behind him, leaving me and Ellie alone in the house. Some of her cousins are getting in later today so this is probably my last chance to talk to her alone before the house starts filling up.

I hesitate on the doorway into the living room, toying with the tinsel framing the door.

"Are you going to come in or just stand over there like a creeper?" Ellie calls. Apparently I wasn't being as stealthy as I thought.

"Sorry" I tell her and go sit down on the couch. It's not the only apology I need to make.

Ellie smiles, "It's fine. I figured this morning would be a little awkward."

"About that," I start but Ellie interrupts me,

"It's fine," She says quickly, "We can just forget it happened"

"Are you sure?" I ask, thankful that she's actually looking at me and not upset or uncomfortable.

"It's not a big deal. I think we can both agree that it's natural that what happened, happened given how close we've been these last few days." Ellie starts fidgeting with her hands, picking at her nails and such. I think she's also referring to the dream she had last night.

"I agree" I say quietly. I want to stop her from fidgeting but I almost afraid to touch her, something I was not aware was possible. Finally, the silence gets to me, the only sound in the room that of Ellie picking at her nails.

"Take a breath," I tell her, "You're going to make your fingers bleed" I place one hand on top of hers and exactly what I expected happens, Ellie tenses up. I quickly pull away and resist the urge to apologize again.

"You're right," Ellie tucks her hands under her thighs, "I think we can both agree feelings have bubbled up that neither of us expected." Ellie glances down at my lips so quickly I almost miss it, and I realize, Ellie didn't tense up because she's disgusted by me, Ellie tensed up because she's attracted to me. It instantly changes the dynamic more than I thought possible.

Her next words only confirm my thoughts.

Ellie nods to herself, "I think we just need to try to keep our hands to ourselves until these feelings wear off" She glances down at my lips again.

"Do you think they will? Wear off, I mean."

Ellie meets my eyes, "We've known each other our whole lives. A sudden burst of attraction doesn't change that."

"You didn't answer my question"

I can almost watch her pupils dilate in real time. Suddenly I'm reminded of her dream last night and the fact that neither she, nor I, ever got full satisfaction from the event. Just more frustration and embarrassment.

"We could mess up our agreement," She tells me, "We put those rules in place for a reason"

I watched her tuck the napkin into her nightstand on the first night. I briefly wonder if it's still there, a physical reminder of what we agreed to.

Thinking about the napkin with our rules on it breaks whatever spell I had fallen into.

"You're right," I look away from her towards the paused television, "We're doing this to fool our parents, to get them off of our backs and to have a peaceful holiday. That is still the goal."

Ellie nods, I can't tell if she's satisfied or disappointed by my words.

"Staying apart it the right decision," I continue, not able to look at her, "If we got involved, it would only be messy and complicate things."

"Exactly, that's the last thing we want. The whole reason we started this was to get some peace."

"It wouldn't be worth it" I finally look back over to Ellie. She responds so quietly that I almost don't hear her,

"Unless it is"

Chapter Seventeen

BENJI

Screaming interrupts our conversation, and stops me from doing something stupid like leaning over and connecting my lips with Ellies.

Two little girls run in, dragging throw blankets behind them.

"Uncle Benji! Come help us with our fort!"

The two girls belong to my sister Elena. I love my nieces more than life itself; I would literally kill someone for them but somehow, they always have the worst timing.

Ellie is getting off the couch and walking into the kitchen before I can ask the girls for a moment. Not that they'd give it to me, they can be pretty demanding.

"Of course I'll help you finish your fort. Why don't you head back home and I'll be over in a minute"

"Okay" They say in unison.

Elena had her first child, Laura, eight years ago. Two years after that was Kylie and last year, right when I thought she might be considering leaving Dave, they welcomed Sasha.

My nieces are some of my favorite people in the world but I wish their mother could see that she could do so much better than their father. Elena thinks that because she has kids with the man, they need to stay together. Nothing quite like single parenting when you have a husband.

Not wanting to leave the girls waiting, I quickly find Ellie in the kitchen.

She spots me instantly,

"We're doing the right thing. Staying friends, I mean"

"Are you sure?"

Ellie nods.

"Alright," I tell her, "Friends it it"

As I walk by, heading for the back door that leads to the path between her family's house and mine, I can't resist stopping to place a light kiss on her forehead. I hear her inhale a breath and then I'm gone, towards the chaos I know my nieces will bring.

It's exactly what I need to get my mind off Ellie, and, more importantly, to convince myself that we are doing the right thing.

***

ELLIE

We are doing the right thing, I know that. But I can't help it if I want to tell Benji to come back and take my clothes off.

Luckily, I'm distracted quickly after his departure. It's not like I won't see him in a little while, our family is barbequing tonight at his parents tonight. Plus, we are staying in the same room. I don't know why I feel like I'm missing him.

My cousin Allie comes racing into the kitchen. Allie is the daughter of my uncle on my fathers side, A man who will be here Christmas Eve. I love Allie dearly and we're very close even though she's ten years younger than me and almost my exact opposite. She is also the cousin who is sharing mine and Benjis bathroom and who is most likely to sniff out our deal.

I did not think about Allie when Benji and I first struck this deal, but now that she's here, I'm realizing she could present a problem.

Allie tends to say whatever is on her mind. It's not that I wouldn't trust her not to intentionally spill our secret, but I could see her accidentally making some quip that blows the whole thing wide open.

"Ellieeeee! I'm so happy to see you!" Allie launches herself at me. I return her hug as tight as I can.

"It's so good to see you too Allie!" I start to let go but Allie grips me tighter.

"Not yet," She says, "It's been too long since we were in the same room together"

I can't argue with that and don't want to, so I simply hold Allie tight until she's ready to let go.

Chapter Eighteen

ELLIE

Allie and I spend the entire day catching up. I'm able to steer her away from most things relating to Benji and focus more on her. I know it's only a matter of time before she demands more answers.

According to her, you don't wake up one day and just start dating your brothers best friend out of nowhere. It's a sentiment I'm afraid some of the others in the family share.

By the time Allie and I are done talking, the sun is setting and everyone is making their way to the Harrisons back-yard for the barbeque.

Allie links her arm in mine as we walk the paved path between the two houses. It's not a far walk by any stretch of the imagination, our parents wanted it that way. But it is long enough for me to realize I should have grabbed a thicker sweater.

We arrive at the Harrisons and Allie immediately wanders off to catch up with some of Benjis family.

Speaking of Benji, I can see him over near the grill with his father. He spots me and comes over. He looks concerned and seems to be in a bit of a hurry.

"We have a problem," Benji tells me, "Let's step out and talk"

I'm instantly on high alert. Everyone around us is acting normal but that doesn't necessarily mean anything.

Before me and Benji can find a quiet spot to talk, Benjis mom walks over.

"Ellie! How are you my dear?" Marsha hugs me as if we didn't see each other earlier today when she came over for lunch with my mom.

"I'm great, thanks for asking."

"How is your bakery?" She knows I don't actually own the bakery, and prefer it that way.

"It's doing good. Hectic this time of year, as always, but I'm glad to be able to get away for a while."

Marsha tsks a little, "I don't know why you don't open up your own bakery. You make such delicious things, you'd surely have a line around the block."

It's a conversation we've had before, and one I really don't want to get in to with Benji standing next to me impatiently tapping his foot. Whatever he wants to talk about is clearly bothering him.

"I prefer to be able to separate work and life Marsha, you know that. I'd never be able to get holidays off, I'd bake a lot less and be more stressed. I'm happy as I am."

"Of course honey, I just want to make sure you're reaching your full potential!"

I smile, "Thank you but I'm perfectly content where I'm at."

Marsha starts to say something again but Benji cuts her off,

"Mom I was actually hoping to snag Ellie for a minute, you understand right?"

"Oh of course! I remember what's it's like to be young and in love." Marsha's tone tells me exactly what she's thinking and it has me blushing, even if whatever Benji and I are about to disappear for is the exact opposite of what she's thinking.

"Did not need to hear that mom." And with that, Benji is dragging me away into his house and up to the room he usually stays in.

"What is it?" I ask as soon as the door is closed.

"My sister doesn't think we are dating and apparently, that's the consensus among everyone but our mothers"

"What?" I snap, I should have expected this. It's like Allie said earlier, you don't just wake up one day out of the blue and start dating someone you've known your whole life and had no romantic interest in so far. The only person that knows I had a crush on Benji when I was younger is my brother and subsequently, the one person we don't have to convince of our ruse.

"I was with the girls earlier," Benji starts, referring to his nieces, "and one of them off-handedly mentioned that they heard their mom talking with Carrie about how skeptical they are about our relationship."

"Okay," I start, "That's not bad if it's just Carrie and Elena"

"It gets worse," Benji tells me, "Then later when I was helping my dad prep for the barbeque, he was asking me all these questions about us. He seemed really suspicious, asking all about your life and when I became interested in you, how we met and all that."

"Maybe he was just taking an interest in his sons life?" As I say it, I know we're in trouble. Tom, Benjis father, does not tend to get involved in his kids dating life.

"He has literally never once asked me a question about my dating life, except once when I was in high school to tell me how to roll on a condom."

I wince, "So what do we do?"

"I don't know" Benji sits down on the bed and I sit next to him. It's silent for a few minutes, giving me an opportunity to check out his room.

His room has classic male bachelor pad vibes. Dark sheets, a few sports posters up on the walls and not much else other than an empty desk and dresser. I know my room at my families house isn't much better, but it makes me wonder if the apartment he lives is the exact same or if there's anything homey.

"Any ideas?" Benji asks.

"Not really," I'm a little afraid to mention my one idea after what happened this morning. We decided to keep things platonic and adding anything physical would likely cross a line.

"So do we just try to get through the holidays without it coming up?"

I shrug, "I guess so. I doubt anyone but our mothers will bring it up and they both seem fairly convinced."

As soon as the words are out of my mouth, Benji's phone buzzes in his pocket. He pulls it out and turns the screen towards me. On it is a notification from a group chat that is clearly with his sisters.

<u>Thing one & two</u>

> Elena: What's going on with you and Ellie?

> Carrie: Yeah are you guys actually dating or just pretending?

"Fuck" I curse softly, "What are we going to do?"

Chapter Nineteen

BENJI

Ellie and I take a few minutes to come up with a plan before heading back down to the barbeque. It's not the best, especially after our conversation this morning but I think it's the only way to convince our family of our relationship.

Someone needs to walk in on us together. And not just together, but intimately together.

I hold my sisters off with a "we'll talk later" text and Ellie and I reenter my backyard. All we need is the right timing to present itself.

"Are you sure about this?" Ellie asks

"No, but it's the best plan we have"

Ellie spots Allie across the yard and goes over to her. For now, we just need to play it cool and pretend like all is well.

Ellie seems to be taking this a whole lot better than I am. She's very collected and doesn't seem nervous at all as she talks with Allie. Whereas I, however, feel like a ball of nerves. I don't want to screw anything up and have this whole thing blow up in our faces.

If I'm being honest, I don't think that's what has me so nervous. Being so close to Ellie, intimately so, is what I think has nerves skating up and down my spine. Especially after this morning.

The fact that Ellie knows I was jerking off to thoughts of her is not helping the situation any.

Finally, dinner is served and everyone sits down to eat in various chairs around a fire pit my parents dug a few years back. My dad sits next to me, thankfully not bringing Ellie up again and Brady sits on my other side.

Both men talk across me, with me adding a few comments here and there. Mostly about the latest sports happenings. I'm not big on any particular sport but I know both Brady and my father are.

I pick at my food, moving it around the plate until it feels acceptable to get up and throw it away. I don't know how Ellie seems so calm, just chatting away with my sisters and Allie.

After tossing out my plate, I enter the house. Both Ellies house and mine are set up similarly, with the back door through the kitchen and the living room down a short hall. All the bedrooms are upstairs which makes for plenty of spaces to hide away down here.

Eventually, Ellie finds me. I've tucked myself into a corner near the bathroom, a likely place for someone to walk by.

"Hey" Ellie says quietly. I return her greeting and pause. I don't know what's wrong with me, I'm usually good with girls. But this isn't any girl, this is Ellie.

"You okay?" Ellie asks, picking up on my nerves. It's dark down this way, the hall light being turned off so I can't see Ellie very well but I can hear her without issue.

"I'm good, just don't know how to start this?"

Ellie laughs slightly, "Have you never kissed a girl before or something?"

I huff, "Of course I've kissed girls, but this is different"

I can't see Ellies facial expression, but I can see her nod, "You mean, since it's me"

"I just don't want to screw this up"

Ellie looks up at me, her eyes rather bright in the darkness, "You won't"

And with that, she kisses me.

I'm only a second behind her, placing a hand on her waist and in her hair and then diving into her.

Ellies lips are soft and supple, easily addicting. She reaches up and threads her hands into my hair. She pulls me closer and lets out a little moan that has me spinning her around to press her against the wall.

We pause for a moment to come up for air,

"Do we just keep doing this until someone walks by?" Ellie asks breathlessly.

"Yeah," I respond

"Okay"

And then we're kissing again. Ellies tugging on my hair and I'm gripping her hips hard. I don't know at what point this moved from a simple kiss to convince our families to being all over each other but I'm certainly not complaining.

Ellie feels like heaven in my hands. We could do this for hours and I still wouldn't have enough.

I reach down and twine one of her legs around my waist, pressing into her.

"Yes!" Ellie moans lowly, leaning her head back against the wall and exposing her neck. I know she can feel me rock hard against her but she's pulling me in, not pushing me away, so I'm going with it.

I pepper kisses down her neck, nipping and sucking as I go. I earn another of her little moans and it may be the best sound I've ever heard.

Ellie slides her hands from my hair, down my chest to the bottom of my sweatshirt. Her fingers hesitantly slip under the hem and begin to explore.

Someone chooses that moment to burst our bubble. I didn't even realize anyone was there until they started backing away.

"Sorry!" Carrie calls, rushing the opposite way, back towards the kitchen.

Mission accomplished, I think to myself, but I don't want to stop. Ellie is so warm wrapped around me, looking turned on and needy.

I gently press my forehead to hers, "Should we stop?" I ask.

"Probably"

I ease Ellies leg back down and step back. When we were talking about this, we agreed to go back to normal after it was done. That's what Ellie wanted so that's what I'm going to give her. Although she looks like she wants anything but for me to walk away right now.

It's hard not to dive right back into her. Even in the low light, I can see how turned on she is. But I don't know if she is actually attracted to me, wanting me in this moment, or if it's just the situation.

"If you still want this tomorrow, you know where to find me"

And with that, I walk away.

Chapter Twenty

ELLIE

Letting Benji walk away might be one of the hardest things I've ever done. I was so turned on, I probably would have came right there if he'd continued. But it's not what we agreed to, and we agreed to just be friends for a reason.

Although that reason is looking rather stupid right now.

The next few days pass in a blur. There's lots of Christmas shopping, gift wrapping and cookie decorating. I can't seem to work myself up to talking to Benji about what happened, or asking for more. So I simply say nothing and Benji does the same.

We see each other before bed and in the mornings, but for the most part, our days don't really involve the other.

The good news is that our plan worked, word quickly spread about Carrie walking in on us "all over each other" so now no one is really doubting our ruse. Brady, the one person that knows we're lying, has been silent about the whole thing but I think he's giving me space to figure out my feelings and I appreciate him for it.

Now, it's Christmas Eve, the rest of our combined families have arrived and both houses are full. There's lots of kids running around and lots of festive music playing. It's hard to think about leaving this after New Years. I didn't realize how much I missed my family until I was smacked in the face with it.

"How are things coming?" My mom asks, walking into the kitchen where I'm pulling a new batch of cookies out of the oven.

"They're perfect!" Cookies are one of the things that continue cooking after you've taken them out of the oven so it's important to pull them right before they're fully done and get them off the hot pan once they are done.

"You've been kind of quiet lately, is there anything you want to talk about?" Mom asks, sidling up next to me.

"Not really, just busy I guess."

"You know you can tell me anything right?"

I pause working with the cookies. I almost come clean right there, about everything. About Benji and I's ruse, about the kiss, about us not talking for the last few days and about my complicated feelings that I can't seem to sort through. But we came up with this plan for a reason, so I don't say anything.

"Of course mom."

"Okay sweetie," She pats my back and reaches over and takes the spatula out of my hands, "Why don't I finish up with these cookies. and you go get cleaned up?" She gestures to the large splotch of flour on my shirt and bumps me to the side.

"Just let me know if you need anything" I call as I exit the kitchen.

I hear mom laugh, "Don't you forget who you got your baking talents from?"

"Dad of course!"

Her laugh follows me up the stairs to my room. It's nice to be able to mention dad and not feel an overwhelming amount of grief, but instead, to laugh.

I don't expect to find Benji in our room but when I open the door, he's sitting on the bed scrolling on his phone.

Now seems as good a time as any to confront the issue I suppose.

"Hi Benij"

Chapter Twenty-One

BENJI

She looks amazing walking through the door. For a second, I don't hear a word she says because I'm too busy taking her in.

These last few days have been torture. I got one small taste of Ellie and now it's everything I can do not to take another one. But she never came to me, never told me she wanted more so I'm trying to be respectful of that.

I get up early and go to bed late to try to limit the amount of time our paths cross. We are sleeping in the same room, living under the same roof and fake dating but there is still space I can give Ellie if that's what she wants. And from her radio silence over the past few days, I'd say that is what she wants.

I finally tune back in to what Ellie is saying when she snaps,

"Benji are you even listening to me?"

"Sorry, what were you saying" I can't exactly admit I didn't hear her because I was distracted by the flour dusting her cheek, so I don't give her a reason.

"Just forget it!" Ellie turns towards the bathroom door and I launch up off the bed,

"Wait, I'm sorry. What did you say?"

I'm gently gripping her elbow and just that small touch, through her thick sweatshirt no less, is sending shockwaves through my body.

Ellie turns towards me, slipping out of my grip.

"We just haven't talked much since the barbeque"

"Yeah, you're right" I tell her, "We've both been pretty busy"

"I know we've been busy but," Ellie cuts off.

"What is it?" I want her to continue, I want to hear all of her words.

"Was kissing me truly so bad?"

I'm stunned silent. Ellie must mistake my silence for agreement because, rather than turning towards the bathroom door like she did a moment ago, she turns towards the bedroom door to leave.

"Wait Ellie!"

"No it's fine," She tells me, only a step away from the door, "We agreed to just be friends and I understand if that's all you want. I'm not upset, truly."

"That's not what I was going to say"

Ellie turns to face me, "Then what were you going to say?"

Her face looks hurt, there's a crease to her eyebrows and a slight sheen in her eyes.

I don't have the right words in this moment, so rather than saying the wrong thing, I show Ellie rather than telling her,

"Ah fuck it" And then I kiss her.

Chapter Twenty-Two

ELLIE

"**A**h fuck it"

Benji is kissing me. His lips are on mine and he's got a hand on either side of my face.

I don't know what I expected when I brought up our distance over the last few days but this is definitely the better scenario.

Suddenly, Benji is pulling away, leaning his forehead against mine and talking,

"I didn't stay away because I didn't enjoy myself at the barbeque, and it wasn't because I didn't want you."

"Then why?"

"Because I knew if I was around you too much, I'd end up kissing you again and I wasn't sure if that was what you wanted."

"Oh Benji," He's been holding himself back these last few days, not avoiding me because of the awkwardness like I assumed.

"I want you to kiss me again," I tell him.

"Yeah?" He's smiling against me. It's one I don't think I've seen before. I've seen plenty of smiles from Benji but not one so full of lust and happiness.

"Yes Benji, kiss me again!"

And then he's moving his mouth against me, backing me into the wall beside the door and showing me, in no uncertain terms, how he feels about me.

"Grab on" He groans between kisses.

"What?" Before I can understand quite what he's saying, Benji is picking me up with a hand under my ass and the other wrapped around my back.

I giggle between kisses as he walks us over to the bed.

Benji sits at the edge of the bed with me on his lap. He's kissing me and pulling at my waist. I want to rip his clothes off right then and there. Instead, I push on his chest enough to get him to fall backwards. Then I'm kissing my way from his neck to the slight bit of exposed chest at his neckline.

"Take this off," I tell him, pulling on his shirt.

"Anything for you" Benji smirks. He helps me get his shirt off his head, exposing his glorious chest.

The Benji I had a crush on in high school had abs from playing sports but this Benji is built like a brick house. He's got plenty of muscles but he's also soft in a few areas, a little extra bulk here and there that tells me for however much he goes to the gym, he also lays around taking in carbs.

His body is the best I've ever seen.

"Like what you see?" Benji's got an arrogant smirk on his face. Rather than answering him, I decide to kiss him.

We're back to making out, grinding against each other and running our hands everywhere. Benji is hard beneath me and it's making my panties damper than I think they've ever been.

Benjis hands are at my hips, gripping me tightly. I pull away from his lips just long enough to grip the edge of my shirt and begin to pull it off.

Benji stops me before I can get it over my head.

"What's wrong?" I ask

"Nothing," He smiles, "I just want you to know that you don't have to. Whatever you're comfortable with is more than enough for me"

My heart melts at his words. Here's this big strong man, clearly turned on and needing relief, and all he seems to care about in this moment is my comfort.

"I want to," I assure Benji.

"Then let's get that shirt off"

My shirt ends up on the floor with his. The only thing separating our upper halves now is my bra and I'm quick to remedy that.

"God you're gorgeous" Benji tells me. He's kissing up and down my neck and driving me wild. We've moved back into a more upright sitting position which has me putting weight directly on Benjis lap where he's hard against me.

"I need more," I moan, going after Benjis belt.

"Whatever you want" He's helping me undo his belt. I can't quite get what I truly want in this position so I climb off Benji and settle on my back in the pillows.

Benji turns to look at me where I'm lying. Normally I would feel vulnerable and exposed but it's Benji, a man who I trust implicitly no matter the situation. And the look he's giving me leaves no room to question how he's feeling.

"Are you sure?" He asks, ever wanting to make sure I'm alright.

"Yes" I nod.

"Okay then," Benji smirks and then stands up off the bed. He turns to face me and slowly starting dropping his jeans. I hear the clack of the belt hitting the floor but I can't much focus on it when he's revealed the large tent in his boxers.

"We can stop at anytime," He reminds me, crawling up on the bed with me.

"I know"

I'm grabbing Benji and pulling him on top of me. His weight is delicious and makes me feels so small and cherished.

Benji has one arm propped up on the bed beside me head and the other running up and down the outside of my thigh, reminding me I still need to get my pants off.

"Take them off" I instruct Benji, trying to unbutton my jeans.

Benji bats my hands away, "That's my job," he tells me, "I take care of you"

I groan in frustration, I want my pants off, now.

"Patience," Benji tsks. He pulls back to watch me for a second before slowly undoing my jeans and pulling them down my thighs. When he gets to my knees, he sits back on the bed to work them the rest of the way off.

Before Benji comes back down overtop me, I'm hit with a sudden wave of self-consciousness.

"What is it?" Benji asks, immediately picking up on my feelings.

"It's just," I pause for a second, "I haven't shaved in a while." That's an understatement, it's like a forest down there.

That arrogant smirk is back in place on Benjis face, "That's no issue. I'm a grown man, a little pussy hair doesn't bother me"

"Are you sure?" I ask

"Ellie," Benji starts, taking on a softer tone "As I said earlier, if you're comfortable, I'm comfortable"

I smile, my ex used to freak out if I hadn't shaved or been to my waxer. It's a stark reminder of the differences between Harry and Benji.

I lean up, intent on kissing Benji. Succeeding, I lock my lips with his and pull him back down on top of me. I push all thoughts of my past out of my head, there is no one else in this room but Benji and me and that's the way it's going to stay.

Chapter Twenty-Three

ELLIE

I'm moaning, griding up against Benji where he's sucking little bruises into my tits when I decide it's time to move things along.

I've got my legs wrapped around Benjis waist, holding him against me. There's not a lot of room between us but there is enough for me to slip my hand down to his boxers and palm his cock through them.

"I want you" I moan. Benji is hot and thick in my hand. I can almost feel him pulse in my hand at my words.

"I want you too," Benji tells me, pausing his ministrations against my chest. One hand moves from gripping my hip to teasing the waistband of my panties.

"I need to get you ready for me" And then he's slipping his hand under the waistband and making contact with my most intimate place.

There's no teasing as he moves his fingers in a circle over my clit. I'm thrusting up into his hand, trying to get any additional friction I can.

"That's it, work yourself against me" Benjis voice is low and gruff in my ear. I can tell he's just as bothered by this as I am.

"Fuck, you're so wet"

"All for you" I moan

Benji continues his circles for a second before sliding lower and pushing two fingers into me.

"Oh fuck" My eyes are screwed tightly shut and my legs are clenching around Benji as he starts moving his fingers inside of me. But it's not enough, I need more.

"Benji," I plead, "I need you inside me"

I'm pulling at his boxers, slipping them as far down as I can get when he leans back. He adjusts so he can slip his boxers the rest of the way down.

"Holy shit" I curse, not meaning to say that out loud. Benji is easily the biggest guy I've ever been with. I don't know how it's going to fit but I'm more than willing to try.

"Like what you see?" Benji is eating up this attention, rightfully so. He's hot and he knows it.

"Do you have a condom?" I ask in a brief moment of clarity.

"Yeah one sec" Benji stands up off the bed and walks to the dresser, gloriously naked. His backside is just as attractive as the front. He rifles around in a drawer for a second before pulling out an unopened box of condoms.

Benji fumbles with it for only a second before the plastic falls away and he's able to open the box and draw out what we need. I use that time to slid off my panties, trying to remember Benjis words about the untamed wild curls between my legs.

Benji walks over with the strip of condoms in his hand. He tears one off and tosses the rest down on the bed.

"Where do you want me?" He asks

"On top" I want to feel crushed, in a good way.

"Alright then." Benji's crawling onto the bed and overtop of me. I take the condom from his hand and tear it open.

"May I?"

"Go for it"

I palm his cock, feeling him fully in my hand. He's so warm and thick that the sight itself might be able to get me off.

I quickly go back to my task before I can get distracted by just admiring Benjis dick.

Pinching the top, I roll the condom down his length.

Then there's nothing left, nothing more we're waiting for. I'm about to have sex with Benjamin Harrsion.

"You ready?" Benji asks me, taking his dick in his hand and rubbing it against me.

"Absolutely!" I capture Benjis mouth as he slowly pushes into me.

"Oh fuck," I groan against his mouth. A shudder rolls through me once he's fully seated.

Benji grips my hip so hard I think he might leave more bruises. I'll be glad to wear them.

"Are you okay?" I ask Benji, turning the tables toward him.

"Yeah" He nods against me, "Just need a minute"

When he's ready, Benji starts thrusting. Slowly at first, but he steadily picks up speed.

He's peppering kisses down my neck and I'm leaving scratches on his back.

God, just the sound of us, of skin slapping together, could flood me.

"What do you need?" Benji pants against me

I bite at his shoulder, "My clit, touch my clit"

Instantly his hand moves from my hip to between my thighs. He's got his other arm propped next to me, using it to keep from completely suffocating me. Not that I would mind. It comes in handy though, when Benji picks up speed and starts his assault on my clit, I grab onto it. Now I've got on hand wrapped around his arm, the other digging into his back.

The headboard is banging against the wall, adding to the auditory sensations. If I was in my right mind, I might be worried about being overheard but I'm pretty sure everyone is out to lunch anyway.

"Fuck, fuck, fuck" I'm so close, my legs are clenching around his waist and my nails are digging even deeper into his back.

"That's it Ellie, come on my cock"

His words send me over the edge. I'm clenching and shaking around him. My orgasm triggers his and Benji finishes inside me, filling up the condom with a few final, shaky thrusts.

"Oh," My limbs feel boneless, my mind floating in outer space. Benji chuckles against me, still inside me.

"Good?" He asks

"Amazing"

Benji chuckles again lowly before reaching down to hold the edge of the condom and pulling out of me.

He flops down onto the bed next to me with a slight groan.

"Good?" I ask, repeating his question.

"The best" He tells me.

Benji leans over and plants a quick kiss to my lips before he gets off the bed, picks up the condom wrapper and heads into the bathroom. He returns with a warm cloth which he uses to clean me up before tossing it away and lying down on the bed with me.

Benji gathers me up in his arms. "Still doing okay?" He asks.

"Mhm," I nod into his chest. My body is all warm and fuzzy, I don't think I could get off this bed if someone paid me to.

"Rest for now, I'll get you up in a little while"

I listen to his words, closing my eyes and nodding off in his arms. We have a lot to talk about, things to figure out, but all that can wait. I don't think I've ever been more content than I am right now, wrapped up in Benji after the most mind-blowing sex of my life.

Chapter Twenty-Four

ELLIE

Spending Christmas Eve wrapped up in a post sex glow is a first for me. Even in past relationships, the holidays were usually too stressful to even think about something like that but with Benji, it feels like the most natural and stress-reducing thing in the world.

Banging around downstairs pulled us out of round three, me having woken up to Benjis light snores. I couldn't resist climbing on top of him and waking him up with my tongue. Round two quickly turned to three which might have even continued past that if not for the noises and yelling going on downstairs.

Benji and I both climb out of bed and toss our clothes back on. The second I try to take a step a delicious ache starts up between my legs. It causes me to stumble a bit. I think I've hidden it well until Benji says,

"Problem?"

"Hush" I lightly smack his chest as I walk past him, still struggling a bit to walk normally, "You know what you did"

I can practically hear Benjis smirk,

"Damn right"

We don't say anymore as we exit and head downstairs. When we get there, we find a scene I didn't expect. Benjis sister Elena is arguing with her husband Dave in the middle of the living room. Even more interesting is that my brother Brady appears to be in the middle of it.

"How long has this been going on?" Dave is yelling at Elena. As soon as Benji hears Dave speaking in that tone, he jumps in,

"Whoa, hey! Don't talk to my sister with that tone"

"It's fine Benji," Elena sighs, "It's not a big deal"

"Fuck that," Benji responds, "He shouldn't be raising his voice at you. You're the mother of his children."

"Yeah a mother who cheats" Dave snarls

"Oh like you're one to talk!" Elena snaps back.

"Why don't we all just settle down," Brady jumps in, "We came over here so you guys could get some privacy, not to have a place to start screaming"

Elena wrings her hands together, "You're right Brady," she turns to me, "Sorry Ellie. We came over because I thought everyone was out and my kids are napping back at our house. We just needed a peaceful spot"

I immediately walk over to Elena and lightly grab her hands, attempting to stop her from squeezing them together so tightly. They're starting to turn white.

"It's not an issue," I tell her, "You're welcome anytime, you know that"

"Thanks" She smiles at me, but there's no light in it.

"Why don't we take a walk" I suggest.

Elena looks over my shoulder at Dave, I also turn back and spot my brother and Benji talking to him quietly.

"That's a good idea" Elena agrees.

We step out the back door, instead of heading the direction that will take us to her parents' house, we follow the dirt path towards the back of the property where an old treehouse sits we all used to play in as kids.

"Do you want to talk about it?"

Elena sighs deep, the kind that comes from true struggling, "I do, I'm just afraid once I let it all out I won't be able to put it back"

"I get that," I tell her, sitting down on the bottom step leading to the treehouse. Elena sits next to me and rests her head on my shoulder.

Elena and I were never very close growing up, she's a few years older than me and we just never clicked as kids. As we've gotten older though, a strong relationship has been built. We talk on the phone every so often. She even came to visit and stayed at my house last summer. It's not that we know every single thing about one another, it's that we don't need to in order to have a good friendship.

"I found out Dave cheated on me about six months ago"

"Wow," I tell her, "That's horrible"

She interrupts me to say, "Please don't ask why I didn't leave him. I've had that conversation with every one who has found out and it's not one I feel like repeating."

"I know why you didn't leave. Because of the kids."

Elena nods against my shoulder, "Thank you for understanding"

"Anytime"

We sit in silence for a few minutes before Elena continues her tale,

"I messed up about a month ago. I'd just found out how deep the cheating went and I was feeling bad for myself."

"What happened?"

"I was staying here actually, I just needed a bit of a break. The kids stayed with me but my mom was here so she watched them one night. I wandered out to the bar."

"Social Hour?"

"That's the one," she laughs softly, "I ran into an old friend there and ended up going home with him"

"Ahh," Things are clicking in my head now, "And Dave just found out?"

Elena nods her head, "Yup"

"Well it's not like he has any room to talk. He's the one that broke the relationship. Now he knows what it feels like to be one the receiving end, even just a little bit."

"I know you're right," Elena picks her head up off my shoulder and puts in in her hands, "It just doesn't feel good to be the one causing harm"

I pull her fingers away from her face and link my hand in hers. I can see a small tear track on her face but I'm not going to mention it.

"I'm sure you're feeling pretty shitty." Elena huffs at my statement, "But it'll get better. If you want my advice, leave Dave. You do the majority of the work for the kids anyways. And besides, we'll all be around to help you."

"Yeah that's what everyone keeps telling me"

"Then maybe it's time you listen."

Elena doesn't respond to me and that's alright. We sit in silence for another few minutes before she stands up, dusts her hands off on her pants and turns to help me up.

"You alright now?" I ask her

"Yeah," She nods, "Ellie, I don't think I've said it yet but I really like you with Benji"

I blush, all the way from the tips of my fingers to my cheeks. "Thanks"

"There's one more thing," Elena tells me on our walk back to the house.

"What is it?"

"I'm pregnant."

Chapter Twenty-Five

ELLIE

By the time we get back to the house, Dave is nowhere to be found but my brother and Benji are starting on dinner in the kitchen. The rest of our families should be filing in any minute so it's perfect timing to jump in and help cook somewhere.

"Anything I can do?" I ask Benji

"Nothing much, I think we've got this covered." Benji uses the spatula to gesture between him and Brady.

Benji looks delectable in the joke chef hat I got him for Christmas, that he snooped and found, and my mothers apron. He's stirring something, what I can't tell, but it smells good.

"Alright" I put my hands up in mock surrender, "I won't complain about not being put to work"

Brady snorts from where he's rifling through the fridge. As I'm turning to head back to the living room, Benji asks,

"Is my sister alright?"

I turn back, "I think she will be. She's a strong woman, you know that."

Before Elena and I separated, she told me that her fourth kid is her one night stands and that no one knows. She asked me to keep it quiet, so I will. When she's ready to tell people her news, both that she's leaving Dave and that she is having another baby, she will. Until then I will be keeping my lips sealed.

"Yeah I know you're right I just wish I could fix it for her"

I smile slightly, "This, Benji, I don't think you can do anything but be there for."

I turn to leave again, but not before missing the way my brother was listening intently to our conversation about Elena.

***

"Dinner was excellent honey" Mom tells Brady as he's taking her plate out of her hands. We're all lounging in the living room with my favorite Christmas movie, How The Grinch Stole Christmas, playing. It's my mom, Brady, Allie and some of our extended family all wearing our matching pajamas. Benji went over to his families house about ten or so minutes ago, after he finished his plate.

It's been a little weird, having Benji be more involved with my families Christmas. In a good way of course. Both families are always mingling, and of course we do our big Christmas dinner and New Years together, but in the past Benji spent most of his time at his parents house. With him and I now 'dating' it brings him over here, and deeper into our side of the family.

I snuggle in closer to moms side, it's times like this when I feel the most guilty about lying to her. But with these new developments between Benji and I, who knows, maybe one day I won't be lying.

Mom strokes my hair right as Max, the Grinches dog, comes on screen.

"How are you honey?" Mom asks lowly.

I look up at her from my position with my head on her shoulder,

"I'm good mom. How about you?"

Before she can respond, a loud clatter comes from the kitchen, followed by a curse and then "I'm alright"

"Brady, language!" Mom yell towards the hall.

She doesn't get a response but I can imagine what Brady is thinking.

We both giggle and tuck back into each other.

"I'm good sweetie," Mom starts, picking up our conversation, "Better with you here"

My eyes get a little misty. Mom is not stingy with her affection but it's hitting harder tonight.

"I love you," I tell her

"I love you too sweetie"

We both fall silent and watch the rest of the movie. Eventually, the Grinches heart grows three sizes and Christmas is saved. I take that as my opportunity to go upstairs and start getting ready for bed.

"Goodnight," I call to everyone still in the living room.

I get a few responses but it's mostly silent. As is mine and Benjis room when I arrive. I plan to wait up for Benji so we can talk but my plans are quickly thwarted by sleep taking me.

Chapter Twenty-Six

BENJI

I like Christmas, it's my favorite holiday, but somehow, this year has been incomparable to years past.

Maybe it has something to do with the angel sleeping beside me. When I finally came to bed last night, after a long talk with Elena, Ellie looked so warm and cozy in bed that I couldn't resist snuggling into her. Waking up this morning, I find that I'm in the exact same position I fell asleep in.

It's the first morning since this whole thing started that I'm entirely comfortable holding tight to her. Even just a few days ago, I would have tried to extricate myself from the bed before she realized how tight my hold on her was.

Now, I pull Ellie deeper into me instead of pushing her away.

"Good morning" she says sleepily, stretching out and pushing her backside further into me.

"Good morning," I kiss her shoulder, "Merry Christmas"

Ellie turns in my arms, "Merry Christmas," she tells me. Then she leans up and places a light kiss on my lips. There's sleep lining her eyes and a slight blush to her cheeks.

"Are you excited for today?" I ask. She mumbles a response but looks rather dazed. She's zeroed in on the stubble from where I haven't shaved.

Before I can capture her lips and make this into the worlds best round of morning sex, our door bursts open and in comes two little bodies.

"Merry Christmas uncle Benji!" Laura and Kylie, my sisters girls, launch themselves onto the bed with us.

"Merry Christmas Kiddos!" I laugh and sit up in the bed. They might have just blocked me a bit, but I know there will be other times and kids aren't young forever.

"Merry Christmas Ellie" Laura says, crawling under the blanket with us. Kylie is sitting on my lap, in the cutest set of Christmas pajamas, but she's not smiling. Beside me, Ellie and Laura are talking quietly.

"What's wrong?" I ask Kylie.

"My dad left"

"What?" For a second, I think I've understood wrong. I know Dave isn't the best husband, and can be a bit of an asshole, but I didn't think he'd leave his kids on Christmas.

"I heard mommy and dad arguing last night. When we woke up this morning, mommy told us he had to leave."

"Oh honey" I wrap my arms around her, I want to tell her I'm sure he had a good reason but I can't seem to force out the words. I don't like Dave, but I've never let my nieces see that. They're so young, only eight and six, they don't deserve this.

I look over and find Laura in Ellies arms, eyes glistening, it's Christmas and kids should never cry on Christmas unless it's tears of joy.

Before I can attempt to bring their spirits up, my sister comes bursting into the room.

"There you are girls! I've been looking all over for you!"

"Sorry guys," Elena says, coming around to my side of the bed, "They ran off right after they finished breakfast"

"It's fine," Ellie says, "They just wanted to say good morning to their favorite uncle"

"He's my only uncle!" Laura insists.

"That doesn't mean I can't be the favorite"

Reaching over, I tickle Lauras belly, getting her smiling.

Laura starts shouting, "Enough!" so I let up on her. But it did the trick, both girls are giggling now.

"How about we go downstairs and open up a few presents" Ellie offers, "I've got some special ones hidden away just for you girls"

Both girls cheer and jump out of bed. They run down the hall yelling about opening presents. If the rest of the house wasn't awake yet, they sure are now.

Ellie smiles at me as she slides out of bed. The way she handled my nieces just now makes me want to drag her into this bed and make them a cousin.

As if she can tell the direction of my thoughts, Ellie smirks, gives me a quick peck and exits the room. As Ellie shuts the door, I turn to my sister. We might not always talk everyday, we might disagree about quite a few things, but she's still one of the most important people in my life.

Seeing the tears starting to well up in her eyes, I quickly climb out of bed and wrap her up in a hug. I hold her until her tears have dried.

CHAPTER TWENTY-SEVEN

BENJI

The events of this morning were definitely the low point. Since then, the day has gotten better and better. Ellie and I are currently in the kitchen, doing some of the prep work for this evenings meal when a loud shout comes from the living room.

"This is a disaster!" That sounded like Celia, Ellie and Bradys mom.

Ellie puts down the whisk she was using, dusts her hands off on her apron and heads down the hall to the living room. I give Allie, who's in the kitchen with us, a quick look before following.

We find Ellies mom in the living room standing in front of the eight-foot Douglas Fir tree. She's got a string of lights in her hands. It doesn't take long to figure out the issue. It looks like a string of the iridescent multicolored tree lights have gone out.

"We can't host with half the tree unlit" Celia states, turning to Ellie and me.

"It's fine mom," Ellie begins, "I'll go up into the attic and grab a new strand. No problem, everything will be taken care of before dinner."

"Thanks sweetie," Celia offers, "But take Benji with you to help"

"Okay mom" Ellie knows better than to argue.

We make a quick stop in the kitchen to leave Ellies apron behind and instruct Allie to take out the pie in the oven when the timer goes off if we're not back before then.

The attic can be found by pulling a string on the second-floor landing, which drops a staircase. Most people think of attics as small and dusty, but not this one. It's well maintained and organized, with rows of holiday stuff down one side and a few spare pieces of furniture down the other. There's a small window of the far side which lets in quite a bit of light and the beams of the ceiling are exposed. Overall, it's actually quite a nice space.

Ellie goes up the stairs first, giving me a spectacular view. Once we're in the attic, it doesn't take long for Ellie to find the box of lights.

I look around the space a bit before eyeing Ellie. She's in tight leggings she changed into a little while ago and an ugly Christmas sweater. It's bright green with tinsel and mini ornaments hanging off of it.

Ellie pulls out a strand of lights and turns to head back for the stairs.

"Wait," I tell her, walking over and taking the lights from her hand, "We should check them first"

"Good idea" Ellie follows me to the outlet in the corner of the room. As I bend down to plug in the lights, I look over at Ellie. She's chewing on her lip, a sure sign she has something on her mind.

"What's up with you?" I ask, straightening with the lit up lights in my hand. They're a perfect match for the burnt out ones on the tree downstairs.

"It's nothing" Ellie says, looking up at me.

"Liar," I tell her and smirk. Ellie's biting her lower lip again so I reach over and pull it loose.

"What is it?"

"We had sex" Ellie blurts, "Really good sex"

"That we did, multiple times" Ellie's comment has already inflated my ego.

Ellies cheeks burn, for a second her eyes go glassy, likely remembering, before she shakes her head and continues talking,

"What happens now?"

"What do you mean?"

"You know what I mean," Ellie rolls her eyes.

"Ellie, are you asking me to be your boyfriend?"

"I don't know" Ellie looks away, toeing the ground. For a second, it was fun to mess with her, but I don't like the nerves playing out on her face.

I take the lit up lights in my hands and loop them around the back of Ellies neck, pulling her closer to me.

"The answer is yes," I tell her, "I want to be your boyfriend Ellie"

"You do?"

"Yeah Ellie," I start, gathering the lights in one hand so I can tilt her face towards me with the other, "I really do and I'm hoping you want to be my girlfriend"

"We still have so many things to figure out"

"I know, but we're both smart people. I'm sure it'll be fine"

Ellie is smiling now, "You're sure?"

"Ellie, listen to me, I'm thirty-five. I've had relationships before but in none of them did I ever feel as strongly as I already do for you. So I'm asking you, plain and simple, will you be my girlfriend?"

Ellies face lights up like the Christmas lights strung around the back of her neck,

"Yes!" And then she's kissing me.

We kiss deeply for a few minutes before coming up for air. We're both smiling and breathing hard. Ellies eyes have that turned on, glazed over look to them that I can't resist.

"Turn around" I instruct

"What?"

"Turn around and put your hands on the wall"

A watch a small tremble wrack Ellies body before she does what I said, turning and placing her hands on the wall.

I keep the lights strung around her neck but as she turns, they cross the front of her neck instead of the back.

With the lights in one hand, I move her hair to the side and pull slightly.

"Oh," Ellie moans. I start peppering little kisses to her neck before moving lower.

Ellies back is to me, but I'd bet that if I turned her around, I'd find that glazed look and a deep crease in her eyebrows.

"What are you doing?" Ellie asks as I get to me knees behind her.

"You'll see"

I finger the waistband of her pants. Working them down with only one hand, so I can keep some tension in the Christmas lights. It's not easy but it'll be worth it.

I bite her hip as I expose it. Her legs flex together, trying to relieve some of the tension. She starts to reach down to help me but I quickly fix that.

"Keep your hands on the wall"

Ellie doesn't respond, other than a small whine, but she does put her hands back where I told her to.

"Good girl"

A full body shiver takes over Ellies body at my words.

"You like that?" I ask, working her pants lower. I've almost got them to her knees.

Ellie nods quickly.

"Use your words"

"Yes Benji, I liked you calling me a good girl"

I give her ass a little slap over her red panties.

"Then I'll have to do it again"

Her panties have little green bows on them which otherwise I would find perfect, but right now, they're just in my way.

I pull them down roughly, jerking her body a little and putting more tension on the lights. They're tight enough against her neck to give a good amount of pressure but not so tight that they'll leave any marks.

I've got her completely exposed now, wrapped up in Christmas lights and panting with her arousal.

Pausing for a second to take her in, I sit back on my heels. Ellie, bent slightly, half naked and waiting on my next move is a sight I'd like to sear into my brain and keep for the rest of my life.

"Benji, what are you," I cut her off by leaning forward and burying my face between her thighs.

"Oh fuck," Ellie yells, I'd be a bit concerned about people hearing us if I wasn't so turned on by the sound. Besides, everyone is on the first floor and you can't hear much from the attic all the way down there.

I tilt my head to give me better access to her clit and earn another moan for my efforts. I'm dragging my tongue through her, nipping and sucking as I go. I keep going until I've got Ellie right on the precipice of orgasm.

She pulls away slightly and one of her hands falls away from the wall to reach back and grip my hair.

"Right there!" Ellie moans. I love seeing this side of her, the side that takes what she wants.

To push her over the edge, I take my one hand from her hip and add my fingers to her clit so I can stick my tongue fully inside her.

Ellie mumbles something entirely incoherent before her legs clench as tight and they can and she comes on my face.

I work her through it until she's full body trembling and collapsing.

Ellie slides down the wall until she's down at my level. She turns and I was right, she's got that glazed look on her face and a furrow in her brow.

"That was," She starts,

"Amazing" I finish for her.

Ellie looks down at my lap where I'm tenting my pants. She starts to reach for me but I gently grip her wrist and stop her.

"Don't you want me to,"

I interrupt, "I'm good"

"Are you sure?"

I nod my head, lean forward and kiss her.

"I've got everything I need"

Chapter Twenty-Eight

ELLIE

If I never move from my spot on this couch, then know I died happily.

After a feast fit for kings, everyone moved to the living room where gifts were exchanged, laughs were had and hot chocolate was passed out.

Buried under my new cozy throw blanket covered in decorative cinnamon rolls, I've got my feet propped up in Benjis lap where he's massaging them gently. We're watching his nieces play with some of their new toys on the carpet in front of us. Elena is passed out on the other side of the couch, Brady and Allie are cleaning up in the kitchen and our parents are nowhere to be found.

"Think you'll be ready for bed soon?" Benji asks quietly

I shake my head, "No I think I'll stay in this spot for the remainder of the trip"

Benji laughs, "Alright then. But how will you open your final present?"

I perk up a bit, "Present?"

"Yeah I've got something stashed away for you in our room"

"Maybe you could just bring it down here, that way I can stay warm and cozy"

Smirking, Benji says, "I don't think so"

"Fine, fine" I start to get up off the couch but Benji stops me.

"Hold on a sec" He slides my feet off his lap and stands. Moving in front of me, he puts an arm under my knees and wedges the other between my back and the couch.

"What are you doing?"

"What does it look like I'm doing?" Benji huffs sarcastically, "I'm carrying you to bed, obviously"

"Benji!" I screech as I'm lifted off the couch. Thankfully I wasn't too loud and didn't wake Elena her sleeping baby Sasha.

"Night girls" Benji calls to Laura and Kylie. They both giggle at the sight of Benji carrying me around but then murmur their goodnights.

Benji carries me all the way up the stairs and into our room before tossing me down on the bed. I bounce and giggle. I think 've had more fun in the past week with Benji than I had my entire relationship with Harry.

Rifling through the top drawer in the dresser on his side of the bed, Benji searches for a minute before pulling out a small, wrapped box. He slides onto the bed next to me and says, "Here"

"What is this Benji?"

"It's a present"

I roll my eyes, "Obviously but when did you have time to get me this? I know you didn't have anything to begin with"

"That's true," Benji nods, "I didn't realize you were coming this year, so I didn't have a gift for you, but the other day mom and I went into the antique store during a grocery run. I found that and it reminded me of you."

I purse my lips, all I got Benji was a joke chefs hat. I would have gotten him something else but I haven't had the time to properly go shopping.

"I know what you're thinking," Benji says, "But stop, I like my hat and I did not buy that to make you feel bad. I bought that because it's beautiful and reminded me of you"

I lean over and give Benji a quick kiss before tearing at the wrapping paper. I pull out a small velvet box and pop it open.

"Oh my gosh Benji, you didn't have to do this"

Inside the box is a small, vintage charm bracelet. The dainty gold chain has a few crystal charms hanging off and gold heart. It feels like entirely too much.

Benji takes the box from my hands and pulls out the bracelet, "It hasn't come in yet, but I found a charm in the shape of a whisk that I think will match the rest of the charms well"

My eyes well up, "Thank you Benji"

Benji fastens the bracelet onto my wrist, "I know whatever we're doing is new but I want you to have a reminder of how much I care about you wherever you go"

A single tear slides down my cheek, "That's beautiful. Do you think you could find me a charm in the shape of the letter B?"

Benji smiles, "Anything for you"

I quickly lean over and kiss the smile off his face. We spend the entire night making love, laughing and smiling.

Best Christmas ever.

Chapter Twenty-Nine

ELLIE

"So Ellie, any New Years Resolutions?" Carrie asks from across the table.

"Not many," I shake my head, "I do want to try to pay better attention to my garden this year and go to the gym more but I'm not very serious about either of those."

A few people around the table chuckle. It's definitely not as full as our table was for Christmas dinner but we've got almost everyone closest.

The past week has been a blur of the holidays, sex and Benji. We went on our first official date the other night, to a small ice-skating rink in the next town over. We've both laughed so hard and smiled so widely, I don't want this trip to end.

I go home tomorrow, Benji the day after. We've talked about how we are going to make it work. Thankfully Benji wasn't kidding when he originally said that his apartment wasn't far from the town I live in. It's about a forty-five minute to one hour drive max.

I'm going to visit him, he's going to visit me. We are going to make this relationship work.

Both Benji and I talked to Brady last night, before he left. We told him our relationship was official now. Although we also said that the way it started, our fake dating scheme, was no one else's business and asked him to keep it to himself, Brady did not have any criticisms. He actually told us that he was happy for us.

I'm a slight bit worried about Brady, he seemed more somber than usual and off. On a possibly related note, I heard Elena is going back to hers and Daves house. Supposedly she is only going to get some of hers and the girls' stuff before coming back here to figure out what's next but no one is one hundred percent sure of that. It wouldn't be the first time she's gone back to Dave after she said she was leaving him.

I have a feeling this time is different, I just hope it sticks.

Speaking of Elena, she's sitting down the dinner table, next to her mom. It's only me, Benji, Elena and the girls, Allie, Carrie, and Benjis mom. My mom is nowhere to be seen, although I know she's in the house somewhere, and Benjis dad had to leave early a few days ago for a work emergency. The rest of both of our extended families have left.

New Years dinner starts to wind down, plates being cleared and drinks being emptied.

I notice Carrie, Benjis little sister, eyeing Benji and I's entwined hands on the table.

"Everything okay Carrie?" I ask

"Yeah," Carrie smiles, "I just can't believe I ever thought you guys were faking it"

Benji squeezes my hand as my face heats. Directly across the table from me, next to Carrie, Allie snorts.

"If you had seen all the condom wrappers in their bathroom trash you wouldn't have any doubts, that's for sure." Allie comments.

My face heats to never before seen levels, Benji chokes on his sip of water and Elenas fork clatters to the table.

"Mom," Laura asks, "What's a condom?"

"Oh my god" I say quietly, letting go of Benjis hand to cover my face.

"We'll talk about it later sweetie" Elena pats Lauras head.

Then, dinner gets even more awkward when Benjis mom says,

"I don't know why you two are still using those things. I could use some more grandkids"

"Not the time mom" Benji says, patting my back.

I don't know how but eventually, the awkward moment passes and dinner resumes. I subtly kicked Allie in the shins under the table at one point but no one else noticed.

My mom gets back right as we start clearing our plates.

"Can I talk to you two?" She asks, voice tight.

"Sure" I tell her, getting out of my seat.

We're in Benjis parents house, not ours, so when Benjis sister starts clearing our dishes claiming that guests shouldn't work, I let her take my plate.

Benji comes up behind me where I'm standing off to the side of the dinner table, a few people still lingering around.

"What is it mom?" I'm starting to get a bit concerned.

"I found this in your room"

Then, my mom crumbles my carefully built reality by pulling out a napkin I had tucked into my nightstand. Not just any napkin, the napkin Benji and wrote our rules on that clearly states our lies and the fact that we were not in an actual relationship.

Chapter Thirty

ELLIE

"What the heck mom?" I snap, taking the napkin from her hands.

"Why does that say you two were 'fake' dating?" She uses air quotes around the word 'fake.'

"What were you doing in our room?"

"I was leaving you a going away present!"

Beside me, Benji hasn't said a word, other than to place a hand on my lower back.

"You didn't have to open up my nightstand to do that"

"That's not the point!" Mom snaps, "Why did you lie? Why did you tell me the two of you were in a relationship when that napkin says that's not true?"

"So you were snooping!"

"What is going on?" Benjis mom, Marsha, cuts in. We've obviously drawn an audience. I can practically feel their stares on my back.

"Benji, Ellie, what's happening?" Marsha asks again.

"Tell us Ellie, tell us why, according to what I found, you and Benji lied to everyone about being in a relationship?" Mom demands. She's more upset than mad but that just makes it worse.

Benji starts to say something, what, I'm not sure because I cut him off.

"Because I couldn't handle you!" I half shout, immediately regretting the words when I see the look on my mothers face. I hear a few gasps behind me, a harsh reminder that we have an audience.

"What?" She reaches for me but I step back. I may have said the words harsher than I intended but that doesn't make them any less true.

"Ellie, you don't have to" Benji places a hand on my arm, trying to comfort me but he's not helping like he thinks he is.

"Yes I do Benji," I look to him, tears in my eyes, "It's time to tell the truth"

"I just wanted some peace for the holidays," I start, "So I told you I was bringing someone home for holidays but that wasn't true."

"Why didn't you just tell me?" Mom asks.

"Because I didn't want to disappoint you, because I didn't want to hear about all the eligible men you could set me up with, because I just wanted a break"

"I still don't understand" Mom states, she has tears lining her eyes but none have fallen yet.

"I ran into Benji on my way into town and we got to talking. The conversation ended with us coming up with a plan so you wouldn't find out I lied."

I look down at the napkin in my hands and smile a small, tearful smile.

"We didn't think everything through, there were a few adjustments and things we hadn't expected but overall, it worked. Everyone believed we were in a relationship"

I tuck the napkin away, "So yes mother, I lied to you, to almost everyone. I couldn't handle the constant reminders about how single I am, the veiled teasing and the nagging about finding a husband during a time I just wanted to be left alone."

The first of moms tears fall, "Well I'm sorry I'm so bad that you had to lie and drag Benji into a scheme to trick us."

She walks away before I get a chance to say anything more. Rather than chasing after her, I walk away too, out into the dark night. I hear Benji start to say something to everyone else in the room but I don't care to wait and hear what he says.

Snow has started to fall, the perfect compliment to my icy mood. I know I shouldn't have lied but I shouldn't have had to either.

Rather than go back to my house, I walk to the small tree-house where I had that conversation with Elena a few nights back. I climb the old steps and fit myself inside where I start to cry, real wet and ugly tears. So many emotions are flowing through me that I don't feel safe to be around anyone.

I sit for ten minutes, crying alone, before I hear a voice from below.

"Ellie come down here" It's Benji.

I stick my head out the small window, "Go back inside Benji. I'm upset and I don't want to talk right now."

"I'm not leaving until you come down"

Knowing he's not joking, I exit the treehouse.

"I know I screwed everything up Benji, you don't have to tell me"

Rather than saying a word, Benji wraps me up in his arms.

"You did nothing wrong," Benji starts, pulling back, "You expressed your emotions. You might have raised your voice a bit but you didn't scream, you didn't say mean things. You simply stated the truth."

"My mom is so upset"

"She'll come around. You have a right to be upset too you know, she was snooping and rather than talk to you privately, she confronted you in front of everyone and didn't even apologize for making you feel the way you did"

"Now everyone knows we lied" I bunch my hands up in Benjis sweater. I don't know why but everything between us feels incredibly tumultuous right now.

"So?" Benji says, "I don't care if they know. In fact, now it's even better. We can tell the actual story of how we fell in love"

I suck in a breath, we have gotten very close these past few weeks but neither of us has actually said those words.

I look up at Benji, questioning.

"Yeah Ellie, I'm in love with you. I started falling the moment you walked into that bar and back into my life. Those in the past might have been stupid enough to let you slip through their fingers, but I won't"

Benji pauses to take a breath,

"I'm in love with you Ellie. I want us to have kids, grow old together, do all the things. We might not be ready for marriage yet, but one day it'll come, as will all the rest but I can't do it without you Ellie. Be with me, for real this time?"

I start crying again, happy tears rather than sad,

"Of course, Benji. I love you too. I want all of those things, and I want them with you."

CHAPTER THIRTY-ONE

EPILOGUE

Ten Months Later

ELLIE

Fall leaves have started to fall in my, or rather, our backyard. There's a slight breeze in the air and inside, Benji is warming up some soup we made last night.

Since New Years, Benji and I have moved in together, him convincing his job to let him work from home rather than commute and me, clearing out space in my closet and all over the house for his things. It hasn't always been easy. Especially that first little while where I was trying to repair things with my mom. But we made it work, just like we said we would.

My mom and I have a better relationship than ever, we had multiple long talks in the weeks following our fight about the way she made me feel, the fact I felt like I had to lie about my relationship and so many other things. Since then, we've had more open and honest talks than we ever have.

A text message lights up my phone and I open it to find it's a picture from Elena, of her three-month-old baby. That's a situation that I couldn't explain if I wanted to. Definitely a story for another time.

"Dinners done!" Benji calls.

I head inside through the sliding door in the back of the house. I find Benji dishing up the soup wearing that chefs hat I got him that he still wears every time he cooks. It's looking a bit worn from all the times it's been dropped in food and put through the high heat cycle on the washing machine.

"Smells amazing" I tell him, grabbing my bowl as I pass by.

We sit down in our living room, forgoing the small dining room table and dig in. The entire meal, Benji seems a bit fidgety. Answering in clipped sentences and bouncing his knee. It isn't until a little while later, during our after-dinner walk, that I find out why.

We're walking, arm in arm, with me bundled up my favorite of Benji's oversized sweaters when Benji stops at one of our favorite lookout points near the house. I go to sit down on the bench but Benji stops me.

"How about we take a picture?" He asks, propping up his phone on the bench.

"Alright," I smile. He's still got that fidgety energy surrounding him. I have an idea why and I'm really hoping it's true.

He gets into position next to me and starts talking.

"Ellie,"

"Yes?"

"We've known each other since we were children, running around and causing chaos. We might not have been very close in our young adult days but we came back together."

"That we did" I'm smiling ear to ear now.

"These last months with you have been the best of my entire life. There have been moments over the course of both of our lives that I think we both assumed we might never get here, and yet, here we are. Two people so desperately in love." Benji pulls a box from his pocket and gets down on his knees.

"Baby, Ellie, this relationship might have started off fake but it's the most realist thing that's ever happened to me. Would you do me the absolute honor of allowing me to become your husband. Marry me Ellie?"

Tears are welling in my eyes, blurring my vision, but I can still see well enough to grab Benjis cheeks and lean down to kiss him.

"Yes, yes a thousand times yes"

***

BENJI

We crash through the front door, barely closing it behind us. Ellie is ripping at my clothes, and I, hers.

"I need you now," she moans.

Were in the hall leading to the bedrooms, I've got her pants off but not her shirt. Before I can work her shirt over her head, Ellie is falling to her knees and undoing my belt and pants, the last item of clothing I'm wearing. Then she's pulling my cock out and taking me in her mouth.

"Fuck El," I lean against to wall over her head, "Just like that"

Ellie works me until I'm almost over the edge at which point I pull her off and toss her over my shoulders.

"Ahh!" She giggles, the sound like heaven.

We make it to the bedroom where I toss her down on the bed and pull off the remainder of her clothes until she's only wearing her charm bracelet, the matching necklace I found online and gave to her for her birthday, and her ring.

I get to my knees at the edge of the bed.

"There's no time for that, I need you now!" Ellie moans

I chuckle, "There's always time for me to spend in my favorite place" And with that, I dive in.

Ellie is moaning loudly and gripping my hair, nearly pulling it out, when I finally come up for air.

"Had enough?" I look up at her

"Never"

I dive back in until she's trembling and clenching her legs around my head. Then I crawl up onto the bed while Ellie scoots back to lay into the pillows. I reach into our bedside table for a condom but Ellie stops me.

"Do you not want to use one?" I ask

Ellie shakes her head, "I was thinking, it probably won't happen right away and we both want kids sooner rather than later so maybe we start going without?"

I grin, I've wanted this for longer than I'd admit but I was waiting for Ellie to be ready.

"Is that a yes?" She asks, giggling a bit.

"Absolutely"

We fuck until we're both sweaty messes and then we go again in the shower. Afterwards, I'm lying in bed, waiting for Ellie to crawl in next to me.

Finally, she exits the bathroom completely naked and crawls under the covers. We're just laying together when I eye the framed napkin on the wall and whisper,

"I'm really glad you walked into that bar"

But she's already asleep so I lay still for a while, simply watching my world in my arms. My whole world changed when I agreed to be Ellies fake date for the holidays, a fake holidate if you will, and I wouldn't have it any other way.

A Note From The Author

Thank you for picking up The Fake Holidate! If you enjoyed, please consider leaving a review on a platform of your choice as it tremendously helps out us indie authors!

Hope you enjoyed!

Sincerely,

Lillie Jean Andrews

Acknowledgements

Thank you to all that have been along for the journey and have been awaiting this new release.

About the author

Lillie Jean Andrews is a born and raised Florida girl. While you might not find her at the beach, she can be spotted at the springs or cozied up with a novel. She loves travel, horseback riding, and has been writing since her early teen years and reading since long before that.

She adores chai tea, cowboy boots, handwritten journals, cypress tree, otters and stickers. She is a mama to one unruly pup named Hannah and although she doesn't always succeed, she tries her best to see the good in each and every day.

Also by

<u>Of Passions and Thrones: A Fantasy Romance series</u>

Book One: The Last Daughter of Smoke and Shadows

Book Two: The First Prince of Pain and Power